VANISHING POINT

Morgan Cipher

Centuria Books

CONTENTS

CHAPTER ONE

CHAPTER 1 – SHATTERED REFLECTIONS

The roses were suffocating me. White as bone, they crowded every surface of the hospital room like mourners at a funeral—thirty, perhaps forty arrangements with edges just beginning to curl and brown. Their cloying sweetness hung in the air, mixing with antiseptic in a nauseating perfume that made my stomach churn. Cards nestled among the thorny stems, each bearing handwritten sentiments in penmanship I didn't recognize.

I blinked against the harsh fluorescent lighting, my vision swimming in and out of focus. The dull throb at the base of my skull pulsed in perfect synchronization with the distant lighthouse beam visible through the rain-streaked window. Three seconds of brightness, then darkness. Three seconds, then darkness. A heartbeat in the fog, marking time in a life that no longer felt like mine.

My fingers found the thin hospital blanket, clutching at its rough texture as if it might anchor me to reality. When I tried to sit up, my body protested with unfamiliar stiffness, muscles aching in places I didn't know could ache. A plastic tube ran from my arm to an IV stand beside the bed, the clear liquid dripping steadily into my veins. I followed its path with my eyes, noting the purplish bruises surrounding the needle insertion site—evidence of previous attempts or adjustments. How long had I been here?

The room spun slightly as I raised my hand to my head, feeling a patch of roughly shorn hair and a line of stitches beneath my trembling fingers. The wound was tender, radiating pain when I pressed too hard.

"You're awake."

The voice came from the doorway—male, cultured, with a precision to each word that spoke of careful consideration. I turned my head slowly, mindful of the throbbing pain.

He filled the doorframe with his presence. Tall, impeccably dressed in a gray cashmere sweater that probably cost more than most people's monthly rent, dark slacks pressed to knife-edge perfection. His face was handsome in a severe way—sharp cheekbones, straight nose, and striking emerald eyes that watched me with an intensity that made my skin prickle. Dark hair swept back from a pronounced widow's peak, touched with distinguished gray at the temples. His hands—long-fingered, steady, unmistakably a surgeon's hands—held a paper coffee cup, steam rising in tendrils that dissipated in the cool hospital air.

"Alex?" The name slipped from my lips without conscious thought, though the face before me remained a stranger's.

Relief flooded his expression, softening the hard angles of his face momentarily before the careful mask slid back into place. He moved toward the bed with measured steps, the sound of expensive leather shoes clicking against the linoleum floor.

"Yes, Emma. I'm here." He lowered himself into the chair beside me, his posture perfect, not touching me though his hands twitched slightly as if wanting to. "Do you know where you are?"

I swallowed, wincing at the sandpaper dryness of my throat. "Hospital," I managed, my voice emerging as a croak. "How long?"

He reached for the plastic pitcher on the bedside table, pouring water with a surgeon's precision. "Seventeen days. You've been in and out of consciousness. This is the first time you've seemed truly lucid."

I accepted the water, careful to avoid contact as our hands made the exchange. The cool liquid slid down my throat, washing away some of the cottony feeling in my mouth. I drank greedily until the cup was empty, suddenly aware of my parched state.

"What happened to me?" The question hung in the sterile air between us.

His jaw tightened almost imperceptibly, a muscle twitching beneath the smooth skin. "There was an accident. On the water. You hit your head." Each sentence clipped, rehearsed, as if he'd practiced this moment.

I reached up again to touch the back of my head, tracing the line of stitches. The wound felt substantial, the area tender and swollen beneath my exploring fingers.

"The doctors said there might be some memory issues," he continued, studying my face with clinical detachment that didn't quite mask something else—anticipation? Anxiety? "What's the last thing you remember, Emma?"

I closed my eyes, trying to push past the blank wall in my mind. Fragments appeared and vanished like half-forgotten dreams—the deck of a research vessel pitching beneath my feet, salt spray stinging my eyes, bright floodlights cutting through darkness, the sensation of falling, water rushing around me, the metallic taste of fear. Nothing cohesive. Nothing I could grasp and hold.

"I was on a boat?" I asked, opening my eyes to find him still watching me intently.

"Our research vessel, yes. The Amphitrite."

The name stirred nothing within me. No recognition, no memory of setting foot on such a vessel.

"What year is it?" I asked, cold dread seeping into my bones.

"2023," he answered. "October 17th."

The information hit me like a physical blow. Five years. A void of five years sat between my last clear memory and this moment. I had been thirty-two, filming a documentary series on deep-sea thermal vents off the Galapagos coast. In my mind, I was still that woman—passionate, ambitious, fiercely independent. Now I was... what? Who?

"We've been married for four years," Alex supplied, as if reading the questions in my eyes. "You're Dr. Emma Walker-Sterling now. We met during your documentary on marine pharmacology. I was a consulting neurologist for the pharmaceutical applications segment."

I stared at him, searching his face for any flicker of familiarity, any spark of shared intimacy. There was none. Just a handsome stranger claiming to be my husband.

"We have a house here in Blackwater Harbor," he continued when I remained silent. "Tidemark. Right on the cliffs, with a private path down to the water. You have a writing studio overlooking the ocean where you've been working on a book about marine conservation and sustainable fishing practices. The photographs you've taken for it are remarkable."

Each revelation landed like a stone in still water, sending ripples of confusion through me. Married. A house named Tidemark. A book project. All unknown.

"And..." His voice softened slightly, the first genuine emotion I'd detected. "We have a daughter. Lily. She's four."

The monitor beside my bed registered the spike in my heart rate with a rapid series of beeps. A daughter. A child I couldn't remember carrying inside me, couldn't remember birthing, holding, loving. The thought was so overwhelming that for a moment I couldn't breathe, my chest constricting painfully.

"I want to see a mirror," I said suddenly, needing to see what else had changed, what other transformations had occurred in the lost years.

Alex hesitated, then reached for a small compact in the drawer of the bedside table. "The doctors said not to overwhelm you, but—"

"Please." My voice was stronger now, insistent.

He handed me the compact, our fingers not quite touching during the exchange. I opened it with trembling hands.

The face that stared back was simultaneously familiar and foreign. My eyes were the same deep blue, but fine lines had formed at their corners. Dark smudges of exhaustion bruised the skin beneath them. My once-wild chestnut hair was shorter now, falling just below my shoulders in controlled waves instead of the unruly curls I remembered. There was a thin white scar above my right eyebrow that I didn't recognize. Most jarring was the expression—guarded, wary, haunted—that I didn't recognize as my own.

"You had your hair styled before the accident," Alex offered, watching my reaction carefully. "You said long hair was impractical with a four-year-old. Always getting tugged or sticky things put in it."

I snapped the compact closed with more force than necessary. "I need to see the medical reports. And speak to my doctor."

"Of course. Dr. Weaver should be making rounds soon." Alex checked his watch—an understated but unmistakably expensive timepiece. "Emma, I know this is difficult. The specialist—Dr. Frost—said your memory could return gradually, with the right triggers. Being in familiar surroundings might help. We could bring you home to Tidemark tomorrow if Dr. Weaver approves."

Home. The word hung between us, hollow and meaningless. I turned away from him to look out the window again. Rain streaked down the glass in crooked rivulets, blurring the view of the harbor below. Through the mist, the lighthouse pulsed its steady rhythm, three seconds of light then darkness. Something about its constancy pulled at me, like a half-remembered song played in another room.

"Those roses," I said, changing the subject abruptly. "Who sent them?"

"I did." Alex's voice softened, taking on a warmth that didn't quite reach his eyes. "One arrangement every day since the accident. White roses have always been your favorite. You find them elegant in their simplicity, you've said."

I frowned, a certainty rising through the confusion. "No. I've always preferred wildflowers. Never roses. The smell makes me nauseous."

The room went very still. When I turned back, Alex was watching me with an expression I couldn't decipher—concern overlaid with something that might have been calculation.

"That must be another memory gap," he said gently, reassuringly. "For our wedding, you carried white roses with sprigs of rosemary. You said they symbolized remembrance and fidelity. There are photographs in your study at home. I can show you when you're discharged."

Before I could respond, there was a light knock at the door. A small face peered around the frame—a solemn little girl with my blue eyes and straight dark hair pulled into neat braids tied with navy ribbons. She clutched a stuffed orca whale to her chest, watching me with an intensity that seemed beyond her years.

"Lily," Alex said, his voice warming with genuine affection. "Come say hello to Mommy. She's awake today."

The child stepped cautiously into the room, her small fingers white-knuckled around her toy. She wore a pleated navy dress with white tights and shiny black mary janes—an outfit that seemed too formal for a hospital visit. She stopped several feet from the bed, maintaining a careful distance.

"Hello," she said in a small voice.

I tried to smile, though my face felt stiff and unfamiliar. "Hello, Lily."

She studied me with that same unsettling intensity, her gaze moving over my face as if memorizing each feature or perhaps looking for something specific. "Do you know who I am today?" she finally asked, her voice barely above a whisper.

"Lily," Alex said sharply, his tone carrying a warning. "Remember what we practiced? Mommy's been hurt, but she's getting better. We don't want to confuse her."

The little girl nodded, but her eyes never left mine. Something in her gaze seemed to be trying to communicate—a significance I couldn't grasp. "Are you still pretending?" she whispered, her voice so low I almost didn't catch the words.

"That's enough," Alex said, standing abruptly. "Naomi is waiting in the hall to take you to the cafeteria for ice cream. Go on now." The firmness in his voice brooked no argument.

Lily backed toward the door, still watching me. Just before she disappeared, she pressed her small fingers to her lips, then turned them toward the window—toward the lighthouse blinking in the distance. The gesture seemed deliberate, meaningful.

When she was gone, Alex sighed heavily, running a hand through his immaculate hair. "I'm sorry about that. She doesn't fully understand what's happened. Children her age can say such strange things when they're processing trauma."

But it wasn't strange, I thought as I turned back to watch the lighthouse beam sweep across the rain-streaked glass. Three seconds of clarity in the darkness, regular as a heartbeat. The child's gesture didn't feel random or confused. It felt like a signal. A warning.

A nurse entered with a practiced smile, clipboard in hand. "Good to see you're awake, Mrs. Sterling! I'm just going to check your vitals." She moved efficiently around the bed, chatting about the improving weather forecast as she wrapped a blood pressure cuff around my arm.

"It's Dr. Walker," I corrected automatically. "Not Mrs. Sterling."

The nurse's hands faltered slightly as she glanced at Alex, who offered her a tight smile.

"Memory issues," he explained smoothly. "Still sorting out the last few years."

"Of course, Dr. Sterling," she said sympathetically. "That must be very difficult for both of you."

I watched the interaction with growing unease. The familiar way she deferred to him, the quick exchange of glances that suggested a shared understanding from which I was excluded.

"I'd like to speak to Dr. Weaver alone when he comes," I said firmly.

Alex's expression remained neutral, but something flickered in his eyes. "Whatever makes you comfortable, Emma. But as your husband,

I'm fully briefed on your medical condition. There's nothing you can't discuss in front of me."

The possessive note in his voice sent a chill through me that had nothing to do with the hospital's aggressive air conditioning. I forced myself to meet his gaze steadily. "Nevertheless, I'd like to speak with the doctor privately first."

After a moment, he nodded. "Of course. I'll wait outside during his visit." He checked his watch again. "I should call the housekeeper anyway, make sure everything's prepared for your homecoming."

The nurse finished taking my vitals, making notes on my chart before heading for the door. "Dr. Weaver will be in shortly. You're doing remarkably well, considering everything you've been through."

When we were alone again, Alex leaned forward, his expression softening. "I know this is overwhelming, Emma. Five years is a significant gap. But we've been happy. Very happy. I have all the photographs to prove it." He reached for my hand, and this time I couldn't avoid the contact without making it obvious.

His palm was cool and dry against mine, the touch clinical despite the intimacy of the gesture. "I've missed you," he said quietly. "The real you. Not the confused, in-and-out-of-consciousness you of the past seventeen days."

I forced a smile, though it felt more like a grimace. "I'm sure it will come back to me. Being at... Tidemark might help." The name felt foreign on my tongue.

"Exactly." His face brightened. "Familiar surroundings, routines, photographs... Dr. Frost says these are all excellent memory triggers."

"And who is Dr. Frost exactly?" I asked, noting how frequently he referenced this specialist.

"Helena Frost. One of the country's leading neuropsychologists specializing in traumatic memory loss. She's been consulting on your case since the accident. You'll start regular sessions with her once you're discharged."

The lighthouse caught my eye again, its beam cutting through the thickening fog. Something about its rhythm called to me, like a half-remembered lullaby.

"The lighthouse," I said suddenly. "What's it called?"

A peculiar expression crossed Alex's face—so brief I might have imagined it. "Blackwater Light. It's automated now, no keeper for decades. Why?"

I shook my head slightly, careful of the pain. "Just curious. It's... compelling."

"You've always been drawn to it," he acknowledged. "You can see it from your writing studio at Tidemark. Sometimes you watch it for hours through your binoculars. You say it helps you think."

Before I could respond, there was a knock at the door, and a middle-aged man in a white coat entered. "Mrs. Sterling! Good to see you fully conscious." He approached the bed with a tablet in hand. "I'm Dr. Weaver. I've been overseeing your care since you were brought in."

Alex stood. "Emma would like to speak with you privately, doctor. I'll wait outside." He touched my shoulder briefly, the gesture possessive. "I won't be far."

When the door closed behind him, Dr. Weaver pulled up a chair. "How are you feeling physically, Mrs.—"

"Dr. Walker," I corrected again, more firmly this time. "My name is Dr. Emma Walker."

He nodded, making a note on his tablet. "Of course. Your husband mentioned memory issues."

"I need to understand exactly what happened to me," I said, keeping my voice low. "And please, I need the unvarnished truth. I have a five-year gap in my memory. The last thing I clearly remember is filming a documentary series off the Galapagos in 2018."

Dr. Weaver's expression turned serious. "You suffered a severe trauma to the posterior cranial region—essentially, you hit the back of your head with significant force. There was substantial swelling, which we've been monitoring closely. The good news is that the latest scan shows the swelling has subsided considerably."

"And the memory loss? Is it permanent?"

He sighed, removing his glasses to clean them on his coat. "Retrograde amnesia following head trauma can be unpredictable. Some patients recover their memories completely, some partially, and some—" He paused, choosing his words carefully. "Some never fully regain what they've lost."

I absorbed this, trying to keep my rising panic at bay. "The accident itself. What exactly happened?"

"According to your husband, you were on your research vessel during an unexpected storm. A wave threw you against equipment on the deck. You were unconscious when the coast guard brought you in."

"Were there other witnesses?"

Dr. Weaver frowned slightly.

CHAPTER 2 - SHADOWS OF TIDEMARK

Alex turned off the sleek black Mercedes and cast a sidelong glance at Emma. "Welcome home," he said, his voice softening with what seemed like practiced tenderness. "Dr. Weaver thinks familiar surroundings might trigger memory recovery."

Emma nodded mutely, her hand lingering on the door handle, reluctant to step out into this life that felt borrowed. The pain medication from the hospital was wearing off, leaving her head throbbing in rhythm with the distant lighthouse beam.

"Need help?" Alex was already at her door, opening it with that same surgical precision that marked all his movements.

"I've got it," she said, more sharply than intended. "The doctor said I should try to do things independently."

Alex stepped back, hands raised slightly. "Of course."

The salt-laden air filled Emma's lungs as she stepped onto the gravel drive, each stone crunching beneath her feet like tiny accusations. She paused, swaying slightly as she took in the full sight of Tidemark—a modern behemoth of weathered stone and glass that seemed to both invite and repel. The massive windows reflected the dying light, turning them into blank, watchful eyes.

"Are you all right?" Alex asked, his hand hovering near her elbow without quite touching her.

"Fine. Just... taking it in." The words felt hollow in her mouth.

The house stood sentinel against the darkening sky, its three stories of calculated grandeur seemingly indifferent to her return. Clean lines and harsh angles dominated the architecture, softened only by the persistent erosion of salt air and time.

"The original structure was built in 1897," Alex explained as he retrieved her small hospital bag from the trunk. "We had it completely renovated after we married. Only the foundation and some interior stonework remain from the original."

Emma nodded again, feeling the weight of his gaze on her back as she followed him up slate steps to a massive front door of polished teak. His keys jingled with an assortment that seemed excessive for a home with presumably only three occupants. The metallic sound jangled against her nerves.

"Seven keys?" she asked, the question slipping out before she could stop it.

Alex paused, hand on the lock. "Security measures," he said smoothly. "The main entrance, back door, basement, safe room, boathouse, garden shed, and my private office. You have your own set—they were in your pocket when they found you."

A memory flickered—keys sinking through dark water, her hand outstretched but unable to grasp them—then vanished before she could hold it.

The foyer opened into a grand entrance hall with soaring ceilings and a floating staircase of steel and glass that seemed to defy gravity. The interior was minimalist, predominantly white with accents of steel gray and midnight blue. Everything gleamed with the immaculate perfection of a space that existed to be photographed rather than lived in.

"It's so... clean," Emma murmured, feeling suddenly self-conscious about the hospital smell still clinging to her clothes.

"Mrs. Winters comes daily," Alex replied. "You were quite particular about the aesthetic. 'No clutter, no chaos,' you always said."

Emma frowned. The words rang false against some buried truth she couldn't quite access. In her scattered memories, she had always thrived in creative disorder—research notes pinned to walls, photography equipment splayed across tables, diving gear hung to dry over bathtub edges.

"Mrs. Winters has prepared your favorite dinner," Alex said, placing her bag on an entry bench. "Seared scallops with lemon butter sauce and asparagus."

Emma's stomach lurched. "I'm allergic to shellfish."

Alex turned, eyebrow raised. "No, you're not. You developed the allergy after Lily was born. Pregnancy can change sensitivities—you researched it quite extensively. We have your EpiPen in every room, just in case."

She stared at him, another disorienting contradiction pounding against her skull. She'd eaten shellfish all her life, had practically grown up on her grandfather's clam chowder during summers on Cape Cod. The memory was vivid—salt air, wooden tables scrubbed pale with years of cleaning, her grandfather's weathered hands breaking open steaming shells.

"I don't... that doesn't sound right," she ventured, pressing her fingers against her temple.

"The memory loss is disorienting, I know," Alex said, his tone gentle but somehow clinical. "Dr. Weaver warned us you might confuse pre-accident memories with childhood ones. Trust me, Emma. I wouldn't risk your health."

His smile never reached his eyes, she noticed. Those remained calculating, assessing her reactions with the detachment of a scientist observing an experiment.

"Lily's with my mother until tomorrow," Alex continued, checking his watch. "I thought it best to give you a night to settle in without too much stimulation. Your neurologist approved the decision."

"Your mother never liked me," Emma said suddenly, the thought surfacing unexpectedly.

Alex's expression flickered—surprise, quickly masked. "That's not true. You two had your differences initially, but you've grown quite close over the years. She's been devastated by your accident."

Another contradiction. Another brick in the growing wall between what she was being told and what some buried part of her knew to be true. Emma wandered deeper into the house, trailing her fingers along cool marble countertops in the kitchen, touching the spines of books in the living room that bore her name on the shelves but contained nothing she remembered writing. On the mantle, framed photographs chronicled the missing years—Emma and Alex at their wedding, her white rose bouquet prominent; Emma visibly pregnant on a yacht; Emma holding newborn Lily with a tired smile; the three of them at various landmarks around the world, always perfectly composed, like magazine spreads rather than candid family moments.

She picked up one frame—Emma and Alex on their wedding day, confetti swirling around them as they descended church steps. Her smile looked genuine enough, but something in her eyes seemed... vigilant. Not the dreamy gaze of a besotted bride, but the careful assessment of someone maintaining appearances.

"You were stunning that day," Alex said, appearing silently beside her. "Everyone said we were the perfect match."

The warmth of his breath tickled her neck, and despite her confusion, Emma felt a flutter in her stomach—the body remembering what the mind had forgotten. His cologne smelled familiar, like rain-soaked cedar, stirring something deep within her.

"Who was my maid of honor?" Emma asked suddenly, stepping away from his closeness.

"Your sister, Caroline. Don't you remember? You were disappointed she left the reception early—food poisoning, apparently."

The way his fingers brushed her wrist as he spoke sent electricity up her arm. Her skin seemed to know him even as her mind rebelled. Emma replaced the photograph carefully. She had no sister named Caroline. No sister at all. An only child raised by her grandfather after her parents died. This fundamental lie made her blood run cold, but she kept her expression neutral, leaning slightly into his touch despite herself.

"Your studio is upstairs," Alex said, following her gaze to another photograph—Emma at a book signing. "The third floor, east side. Best view in the house—you insisted on it for your writing space." His voice softened. "You said the sea inspired you. That you needed it like air."

Without waiting for him, Emma climbed the floating staircase, her hand gripping the steel rail as vertigo momentarily swept through her. The second floor contained their bedroom—a pristine space of white linens and navy accents that felt like a high-end hotel suite—yet the rumpled pillows on one side suggested nights of restless sleep. Had she lain there with him, moonlight casting silver patterns across their skins?

Lily's room was decorated in pale pink and navy with nautical touches, the air tinged with the sweet scent of baby shampoo and talcum powder.

She paused at the doorway, something tugging at her heart despite the memory void. A small bed with a canopy, shelves lined with books and toys, a rocking chair by the window. On the dresser sat a snow globe containing a miniature lighthouse. Emma picked it up, shaking it gently to set the glittering snow in motion. The glass felt cool against her fingertips, the tiny lighthouse spinning in its private storm.

"She's obsessed with that thing," Alex remarked from the hallway, moving closer until his chest almost touched her back. "Takes it every-where. My mother gave it to her for her fourth birthday."

Emma set it down carefully, noticing a small, handwritten card tucked beneath it. She slipped it out when Alex turned away, glancing at the childish scrawl: *For Mommy. When you see the lighthouse, remember our secret. Love, Lily*

Her throat tightened as she slipped the card into her pocket, in-stinctively knowing it should remain hidden from Alex. His hands rested briefly on her shoulders, strong and possessive, before sliding down to her waist.

"You were always a wonderful mother," he whispered, his lips graz-ing her ear. "Lily adores you."

The third floor was accessed by another, narrower staircase. At the top, a short hallway led to a single door. She pushed it open and stepped into a large, octagonal room with windows on five sides, offer-ing a panoramic view of the rocky coastline and the endless gray-blue of the Atlantic. The lighthouse stood sentinel in the distance, its beam sweeping over the darkening waters like a lover's caress across familiar skin.

Unlike the rest of the house, this room felt lived in. Books on marine biology and conservation lined built-in shelves. A large desk positioned to face the ocean held a laptop, camera equipment, and scattered notebooks. Maps and charts covered one wall, with red pins marking locations across the world's oceans. A worn leather chair sat near the largest window, a faded throw blanket draped over one arm.

"This feels more like me," Emma murmured, running her fingers over the desk's surface, feeling the indentations of words written with too much pressure.

"It should. You spend more time here than anywhere else in the house," Alex said from the doorway, his silhouette dark against the hallway light. "Sometimes you sleep up here when you're working late. I find you curled in that chair more often than I'd like." His voice held a note of longing. "Many nights I've carried you to bed, your body warm and heavy with sleep."

The chair. Something about it called to her, beyond mere comfort. She approached it slowly, noting its precise position facing the lighthouse rather than the desk or the sweeping ocean view. Had she sat here night after night, watching for something specific?

"What am I working on?" she asked, running her hand along the leather armrest, feeling the cracks and worn patches.

"Your new book. A comprehensive study on North Atlantic marine conservation efforts. Your publisher is being quite understanding about the deadline extension, given the circumstances."

Emma moved around the room, touching objects, opening drawers, searching for something—anything—that might spark recognition. A collection of seashells arranged on a shelf. A framed photograph of a younger Emma underwater, surrounded by a school of barracuda. Her old diving knife, mounted in a shadow box.

She paused at the knife display. "This was a gift from my grandfather."

"Yes," Alex nodded, moving closer until she could feel the heat radiating from his body. "You insisted on keeping it displayed, though I suggested storing it with your diving equipment. Sentimental value, you said." His fingers traced the line of her jaw, sending a shiver down her spine. "Your passion for the ocean was one of the first things that made me fall for you."

"Why would I mount it? I always kept it functional." Another discordant note in this carefully composed symphony of her supposed life.

"I'll let you reacquaint yourself," Alex said, checking his watch again. "Dinner in an hour?" His eyes lingered on her mouth, as though remembering the taste of her.

When she nodded, he disappeared down the stairs, his footsteps fading. Emma waited, counting silently to thirty before moving swiftly to the door and closing it. She pressed her ear against the wood, listening for any sound of Alex's return. Hearing nothing, she turned back to the room with new purpose.

She crossed to the shadow box and carefully lifted it from the wall. The backing was secured with four small screws. No tools in sight. She glanced around, then removed a letter opener from the desk drawer, using its tip to loosen each screw. The backing came free, revealing the knife still in its sheath—functional, not merely decorative as the display suggested.

Emma removed it, testing its weight in her palm. The familiar handle, worn to the contours of her hand, triggered a flash of memory—using this same knife to cut through fishing line entangling a sea turtle off the coast of Thailand. With careful movements, she unsheathed the blade, finding it clean and sharp. She resheathed it and slipped it into the waistband of her pants at the small of her back, replacing the empty shadow box on the wall.

The lighthouse beam swept through the darkening room, illuminating her face for a heartbeat. In that flash of light, she felt certainty bloom within her chest: whatever relationship she had with the handsome man downstairs, it was built on sand, not stone. And the tide was coming in. Emma sank into the leather chair, staring out at the lighthouse. Its steady pulse seemed to call to her, three seconds of light followed by darkness, over and over. She closed her eyes, allowing the rhythm to wash over her.

One-one-thousand, two-one-thousand, three-one-thousand. Darkness. One-one-thousand...

The counting soothed her fractured thoughts, bringing clarity. Something wasn't right. The studio felt genuine in a way the rest of the house didn't, but even here, inconsistencies nagged at her. The chair faced the lighthouse, not the desk—positioned for watching rather than working. The throw blanket was well-worn but smelled of fabric freshener, as if it had been recently laundered. And beneath the professional camera equipment, she noticed an older model, its case scuffed from years of use. This was the camera she remembered—her documentary camera that had been with her from Thailand to Tonga, capturing coral bleaching and illegal fishing operations.

"Who am I watching for?" she whispered to herself, eyes fixed on the rhythmic sweep of the lighthouse beam. Not what, but who. The thought came with certainty, though she couldn't explain it.

Emma rose, moving to the desk. She opened drawers methodically, finding research notes in her handwriting but with unexplained gaps in dates. The laptop was password protected, and after three failed attempts, she gave up. Her fingers traced the edge of the desk, feeling a slight irregularity in the wood grain. She knelt, examining the underside, and found a small key taped beneath the writing surface.

Standing, she surveyed the room again with new awareness. If she had something to hide, where would she put it? The bookshelves revealed nothing unusual. The closet contained only extra office supplies and research equipment. She moved toward the windows, examining the window seats. Finding nothing, she turned her attention to the floor.

The wooden planks were weathered oak, supposedly salvaged from a shipwreck according to an informational card beside a small model ship on one shelf. Emma walked the perimeter of the room, her footsteps revealing nothing unusual until she reached the area in front of the chair facing the lighthouse. There, almost imperceptible, came a different sound—slightly hollow.

Kneeling, she examined the floorboards more closely. One plank appeared identical to the others but had the faintest line around its edges. Emma pressed and prodded until she felt a slight give. Using her fingernails, she managed to lift the edge just enough to grip it. The board came free, revealing a narrow space beneath.

Heart pounding, Emma reached into the cavity and felt something wrapped in waterproof cloth. She withdrew the package and carefully unwrapped it, revealing a bundle of letters tied with faded blue ribbon. Each envelope was addressed in her own handwriting to "My Lighthouse." None were sealed, suggesting they were copies or drafts rather than sent correspondence.

With trembling fingers, Emma untied the ribbon and opened the first letter, dated just seven months ago.

My Lighthouse,

The waters grow more dangerous every day. He's monitoring my medication personally now, insisting on watching me take each pill. When I "accidentally" dropped one down the sink yesterday, his reaction confirmed my suspicions—these aren't just anti-anxiety medications. Something in them makes time slip away, makes my thoughts fuzzy around the edges.

I've started pretending to swallow, then retrieving them later. My mind is clearer already. The dreams are coming more frequently—not dreams at all, but memories trying to surface. I remember the argument on the boat, the syringe, the lightning. I remember your face as you pulled me from the water that first time. You called me your "drowning siren," and I called you my lighthouse—the steady beam that would always guide me home.

I'm keeping record of everything now, hidden where he won't think to look. If something happens to me, find the manuscript. It contains everything—not as fiction as he's been led to believe.

Three weeks until the new moon. Be ready. I'll signal from the studio window when it's time.

Forever yours in truth,

E

The words sent a wave of cold clarity through Emma's body. Her hands shook as she opened the second letter, then the third. Each contained fragments of a relationship with someone identified only as "My Lighthouse," details of apparent surveillance and manipulation by Alex, and increasingly desperate plans for escape.

The fourth letter mentioned Lily directly: *She draws lighthouses constantly. He thinks it's just a childhood fascination, but she's smarter than either of us at hiding things. Yesterday she asked if we could "visit the lighthouse man" again. I pretended I didn't understand, but later she slipped me a drawing—three stick figures in a boat heading toward the light. She remembers him, even though Alex swears they've never met.*

Emma pressed the letter to her chest, a fierce protectiveness surging through her for this child she couldn't remember raising but felt connected to on some primal level. The snow globe. The secret note. It all aligned with these hidden letters.

The final letter, dated just three days before her "accident," was the most chilling.

My Lighthouse,

He knows. Not everything, but enough to be dangerous. I found him in my studio yesterday, using my computer. When questioned, he mentioned wanting to surprise me by sending my "novel" to his publishing contacts. We both know what he was really looking for.

I've moved everything important to the secondary location. The manuscript is with N now—she'll keep it safe until we're away. I've told Lily stories about the lighthouse keeper who rescues people lost at sea. She understands more than he gives her credit for.

I won't risk writing again before I leave. Watch for my signal tomorrow night. Once he's asleep, I'll meet you where the tide pools form a question mark. From there, we follow the plan.

If I don't arrive by midnight, something has gone wrong. In that case, take what N has and go to the authorities immediately. Don't try to come for me—it's what he'd expect.

Remember your promise: Lily first, always.

All my heart,

E

Emma sat back on her heels, the letters scattered around her like fallen leaves. Cold sweat beaded on her forehead despite the room's comfortable temperature. These weren't the writings of a contented wife working on a marine conservation book. They were the desperate communications of a woman planning to flee with her daughter—a woman who feared her husband, a woman who loved someone else.

Her fingers traced the signature. E. Her own initial, yet these memories felt both foreign and achingly familiar, like a song she once knew by heart but could now only hum fragments of. The lighthouse keeper. The man who had pulled her from the water. The man she apparently loved enough to risk everything for.

Outside the window, the lighthouse beam swept across the darkening waters, steady and unwavering. Three seconds of light. Three seconds of clarity in the darkness. Emma gathered the letters, carefully retying them with the blue ribbon. Whoever this lighthouse man was, he was waiting for a signal that never came.

"I'm here," she whispered toward the distant tower, though she knew her words couldn't reach across the bay. "I'm still here."

CHAPTER 3 - WHISPERS IN THE NIGHT

E mma lay rigid beneath the unfamiliar weight of expensive bedding, eyes fixed on the ceiling. She had feigned sleep when Alex came to bed, maintaining the steady breathing of slumber as he pressed his lips to her temple and whispered endearments that felt like threats. Now, hours later, his sleeping form lay beside her—close enough to touch, yet separated by an unbridgeable void of secrets and suspicion.

The moonlight filtered through the half-drawn curtains, casting silver shadows across the room that seemed to writhe and twist with each passing cloud. Emma watched them dance across the pristine white ceiling, her mind a tumult of half-formed memories and nagging doubts. The letters she'd discovered remained secured beneath the loose floorboard in her studio, but their contents had burned into her memory. Her own handwriting. Her own desperate plans. Her own love for someone who wasn't the man sleeping beside her.

She turned her head slightly, studying Alex's profile in the dim light. His features, so classically handsome they might have been carved from marble, betrayed nothing in sleep. The gentle curve of his mouth, which smiled so convincingly for colleagues and friends, now rested in neutral repose. No hint of the calculation she'd glimpsed behind his eyes when he thought she wasn't looking.

"Who are you?" Emma mouthed silently, her lips barely moving. "Who am I to you?"

The clock's digital display shifted: 2:17 AM.

As if synchronized to that exact moment, her phone vibrated on the nightstand. Emma froze, heart hammering against her ribs. The screen illuminated the darkened room with ghostly blue light. No caller ID.

She glanced at Alex. His chest rose and fell in the deep, even rhythm of true sleep. With trembling fingers, Emma reached for the phone, sliding it carefully from the nightstand. She answered without speaking, pressing the device to her ear.

At first, only silence greeted her. Then—breathing. Low and measured, neither male nor female, but purposeful. Behind it, the unmistakable sound of waves breaking against rock, different from the distant crash beneath Tidemark. Closer. Intimate. As though someone stood on a shore, phone held toward the surf.

"Who is this?" Emma whispered, her voice barely audible.

The breathing continued, unwavering. Ten seconds. Fifteen. The sound wrapped around her like an embrace, strangely comforting despite its mystery. Then, just as Emma prepared to speak again, three distinct taps against the phone's microphone. Deliberate. A signal.

Three seconds of sound. Like the lighthouse beam.

The line went dead.

Emma stared at the phone, adrenaline coursing through her veins. This wasn't the first call. Not according to the call history she'd checked earlier—identical calls at exactly 2:17 AM for the past five nights since her return from the hospital. All from the same unlisted number. All lasting less than a minute.

Alex stirred beside her, mumbling something unintelligible before settling again. His hand reached out in sleep, coming to rest on the sheet between them—a bridge Emma couldn't bring herself to cross. She carefully replaced the phone on the nightstand, her mind racing. The call wasn't random. The timing, the sounds, the three taps—all deliberate communication from someone who knew she'd be awake, who knew she needed to hear those specific sounds.

My Lighthouse, she thought, the phrase from her letters rising unbidden.

The words unlocked something within her—not a memory precisely, but an emotion. A yearning so intense it felt like physical pain, centered in her chest. Something waited for her beyond these walls, beyond this life of elegant confusion. Someone waited. Sleep was impossible now. Emma slipped from the bed with practiced caution, retrieving the knife from beneath her pillow where she'd hidden it after dinner. The cool handle against her palm provided an anchor of certainty in her increasingly unstable reality.

She padded silently from the bedroom, pausing in Lily's empty doorway. Tomorrow—no, today—the child would return from her grandmother's house. The daughter she couldn't remember but who apparently remembered everything, including a lighthouse keeper Alex claimed never existed.

Emma pushed open the door to Lily's room, letting the soft night-light illuminate the space. A child's sanctuary, meticulously decorated in shades of lavender and cream. Stuffed animals arranged in careful rows, books alphabetized on custom shelves. Too perfect. Too orderly for a five-year-old's domain. Emma ran her fingers along the bookshelf, noticing the absence of any stories about lighthouses or the sea. Strange, for a child raised in a coastal home.

She opened the closet door, searching through neat stacks of clothing and toys. At the back, behind a basket of winter accessories, Emma found a small metal lunchbox with a faded mermaid design. Inside lay a collection of crumpled drawings—all of the same subject. A lighthouse. A tall figure with dark hair. A smaller figure that must be Lily, holding the man's hand.

"Who are you?" Emma whispered, tracing the crude but distinct scar on the man's face in one drawing. "Why does she hide you from her father?"

Her fingertip lingered on the paper, as if touch might summon memories. Something about the rough crayon strokes awakened a flutter in her chest—the man's stance, the way he bent slightly toward the child figure. Protective. Loving. Her heart quickened, responding to something her mind couldn't grasp.

She replaced the drawings carefully, ensuring the lunchbox looked undisturbed. Whatever relationship existed between Lily and this lighthouse keeper, the child had instinctively known to keep it secret from Alex. The thought sent a chill through Emma. What kind of man inspired such caution in his own daughter?

Emma continued up the narrow stairs to her studio, each step calculated to avoid the creaks she'd mentally mapped during her earlier exploration. Inside, she closed the door soundlessly and crossed to the desk, removing a small flashlight from the drawer.

Rather than retrieving the letters again, Emma opened her laptop. The password protection had defeated her earlier, but something told her to try once more. Her fingers hovered above the keyboard as she considered possibilities. Her birthday? Too obvious. Lily's birthday? She didn't even know when that was. The lighthouse?

On impulse, she typed: MYLIGHTHOUSE

Access denied.

Emma frowned, considering. If she were hiding something from Alex, she'd choose something he wouldn't guess. Something personal but not obvious. Something connected to...

She typed: DROWNINGSIREN

The screen unlocked.

"Yes," Emma whispered, a small victory in the darkness. The desktop appeared, filled with research folders labeled by oceanic region and conservation topic—exactly what Alex had described as her current work. But Emma ignored these, searching instead for anything hidden, anything personal.

In the applications folder, she found what she was looking for: a custom journaling program labeled innocuously as "Research Notes: Baltic Sea Acidification." She opened it to find dozens of dated entries. The most recent was from three days before her "accident."

Emma began reading, and as she did, the scattered pieces of her life began to form a pattern, like stars aligning into a constellation she'd once known by heart.

April 15 – Alex increased my dosage today. Claims it's for "breakthrough anxiety" but the timing is suspicious. I mentioned wanting to take Lily to the lighthouse museum and he immediately suggested I needed medication adjustment. Pattern continues: any mention of the lighthouse triggers medical intervention. For documentation: new pills are round, pale blue, no markings. Effects include mild disorientation, increased suggestibility, and most alarmingly, memory gaps of 2-3 hours.

*April 18 – Confirmed my suspicions about the medication. Collected samples from three different days and had Naomi run preliminary analysis at university lab. Contains compound similar to experi-

mental memory-altering drug Alex's research team has been developing. Cross-referenced with files from his home office (accessed while
he was at hospital board meeting). Ethical review board denied human
trials six months ago, citing "significant concerns about application
and potential for abuse." Coincides exactly with when my "anxiety
attacks" began.*

Emma's breath caught in her throat, a wave of nausea rising as the
implications settled over her. She was not sick. She was not unstable.
She was being systematically drugged by the man who claimed to
love her, the man who now controlled every aspect of her fractured
existence.

Her hands trembled as she continued reading, each entry more
disturbing than the last.

*April 20 – Lily drew another lighthouse picture at preschool.
Teacher mentioned to Alex, who explained away as "fascination with
our local landmark." Lily later told me secretly that the lighthouse man
has "sad eyes and a hurt face" and that she promised not to tell daddy
about him. Need to be careful—Alex is now checking her backpack
daily, removing any lighthouse drawings.*

*April 23 – Located missing manuscript pages! Alex didn't find
them all. Marcus has agreed to keep them secure with evidence we've
gathered. Meeting him tonight at our usual place to finalize escape
plans. Three more days until we can leave safely. Have secured new
identities and arranged passage on research vessel leaving for marine
sanctuary in New Zealand. Alex will be at medical conference in
Boston—perfect window of opportunity.*

*April 24 – Something is wrong. Alex cancelled Boston trip unex-
pectedly. Claims hospital emergency but called hospital—no emergency requiring neurosurgery consult. Found him in my studio when
I returned from grocery store, using my laptop. Claims he was "check-

ing email" but his expression was wrong. Started experiencing dizziness at dinner—suspect he's drugging my food now, not just medication. Must warn Marcus—*

The entry ended abruptly. The next day was when her "accident" had occurred. Emma pressed her hand against her mouth, stifling the scream that threatened to escape. This wasn't just manipulation. This was calculated. Premeditated. The man sleeping peacefully two floors below had orchestrated the systematic destruction of her memory, her identity, perhaps even attempted to kill her.

And who was Marcus? The name flowed through her veins like warm honey, familiar and sweet. A hidden memory stirred—warm hands, a gentle touch, eyes that saw her true self. Someone Alex feared, someone Emma had trusted enough to plan an escape with—someone connected to the lighthouse.

The knife in her hand seemed to pulse, as if alive with the truth she was uncovering. Whoever Marcus was, he was worth risking everything for. Worth planning an escape. Worth hiding evidence. Worth remembering, even when everything else had been stolen from her. Emma's hands shook as she opened a new entry and began typing.

May 5 – I don't remember writing the previous entries, but I recognize my thought patterns, my phrasing. Evidence suggests I've been subjected to memory manipulation by my husband, Dr. Alexander Sterling. I awoke in hospital with five-year memory gap, conveniently erasing: (1) my meeting someone named Marcus, (2) discovering Alex's unethical research, (3) planning escape with Lily.

Inconsistencies I've noted since returning to Tidemark:

- Alex claims I have shellfish allergy developed after Lily's birth. Family photos show me eating seafood throughout childhood.

- Claims I have sister named Caroline who was maid of honor at wedding. I am an only child raised by grandfather after parents' death.

- Claims I prefer white roses. Have always loved wildflowers, especially blue lupine.

- Claims Lily has never met "lighthouse keeper." Child's drawings and secret note suggest otherwise.

- Mysterious phone calls at exactly 2:17 AM—sound of waves, breathing, three taps.

Working theory: Alex is using me as unauthorized test subject for memory manipulation research. Purpose unclear, but appears designed to create false narrative of our relationship. Possible motives: (1) covering up research violations, (2) preventing my leaving with evidence and/or Lily, (3) pathological need for control.

Priority: Locate Marcus. Determine what happened night of "accident." Protect Lily at all costs.

Emma saved the entry, hiding it within nested research folders, then created a decoy entry about Baltic Sea acidification in case Alex checked the timestamps. Her mind felt razor-sharp, as though someone had wiped clean a foggy window, revealing the stark landscape beyond.

She moved to the window facing the lighthouse, its beam cutting through the darkness. Light swept over her face—three seconds bright, three seconds dark. A rhythm as steady as a heartbeat.

Through the glass, Emma could see the tower's silhouette against the night sky. So close yet unreachable from this beautiful prison. The man who claimed to be her husband slept downstairs, while somewhere near that distant beacon waited someone who had risked everything for her.

Marcus. His name threaded through her hidden journal entries, yet she couldn't picture his face. Only a feeling remained—warmth, trust, and something deeper that made her pulse quicken. A yearning that her lost memories couldn't erase.

The phone calls at 2:17. The three taps. A signal she was meant to return before her "accident." Someone watching, waiting for her all this time.

Emma pressed her palm against the cold glass, aligning her hand with the distant beam as it swept past. Three seconds of brilliance. Three seconds of clarity in the darkness.

"I need to find you," she whispered toward the lighthouse. "I need to remember."

She checked the desk clock: 3:42 AM. Hours before Alex would wake, before Lily would return from her grandmother's house. Time enough to search, to piece together fragments of the life she'd apparently tried to flee.

Emma returned to the laptop, methodically examining files and folders. Most contained exactly what they claimed—research notes, conservation data, draft chapters for Alex's marine biology book. Nothing suspicious or revealing.

Until she found it—a folder labeled "Blackwater Lighthouse Historical Society" filled with hundreds of photographs. Not historical images but recent ones. The lighthouse. The keeper's cottage. The rocky path winding from beach to tower. Close-ups of tide pools forming a question mark when viewed from above.

And in the final subfolder, photographs of a man.

Tall, broad-shouldered, with a weather-worn face that spoke of days spent under open sky. Dark hair tousled by wind, strong jaw marked by a jagged scar running from ear to chin. But his eyes captured her—intense, clear blue like deep water, gazing directly at the camera with such raw tenderness that Emma couldn't breathe.

The photograph had been taken at sunset, golden light warming his features, softening the harsh line of his scar. He stood on the rocks below the lighthouse, one hand extended toward the camera as if reaching for the person behind it. For her.

She knew those eyes. Knew the rough texture of that scarred jawline beneath her fingertips, the timbre of his voice against her ear, the strength in those hands pulling her from dark waters.

"Marcus," she whispered, the name like honey on her tongue.

The image blurred as unexpected tears welled in her eyes. This was the man from her letters. The lighthouse keeper. The one she had risked everything for, who had promised to help her escape with Lily.

Emma touched the screen, tracing the line of his scar. Unlike the polished perfection of her life with Alex, this man's face held character, history, truth. The jagged mark told a story of survival, of pain endured and overcome.

"I loved you," she murmured, certainty blooming inside her like warmth. "I still—"

A soft creak from the stairway froze her in place. Emma quickly closed the laptop, plunging the room into darkness broken only by the sweeping lighthouse beam. She held her breath, knife clutched in her hand.

Silence. Then another creak, further down. Retreating.

Emma exhaled slowly, her heart hammering. Alex, checking on her? She couldn't risk discovery, not now when she was finally grasping the truth.

She waited ten minutes, counting the lighthouse beam's revolutions, before silently making her way downstairs. The hallway stood empty, shadows pooling in corners. Emma paused outside the master bedroom, listening to Alex's even breathing before slipping inside and returning to her side of the bed.

As she lay in the darkness, knife hidden beneath her pillow, Emma stared at the ceiling and made a silent promise to the man whose face she now remembered, whose name felt right in her damaged mind.

I will find you. I will remember everything. And we will finish what we started.

She let her fingers drift toward the window, where the lighthouse beam swept through the night. With each flash, Emma felt something strengthen within her—not memory exactly, but something more basic. A bond that Alex's chemical tricks couldn't touch. A truth her heart recognized even when her mind could not.

Outside, the lighthouse beam continued its eternal sweep, three seconds of light cutting through the darkness.

Three seconds of truth in a world built on lies.

Tomorrow, Lily would return. Tomorrow, Emma would carefully discover what the child knew, what the child remembered. Tomorrow would bring her one step closer to the lighthouse, to Marcus, to freedom.

For now, she would wait, counting the flashes against the darkness. One, two, three.

Truth, truth, truth.

CHAPTER FOUR

CHAPTER 4 - ECHOES OF TERROR

Emma stood before the bathroom mirror, fingertips tracing the small crescent-shaped scar above her left eyebrow—a mark Alex claimed came from a childhood fall, though the tissue felt fresh, still pink and tender to the touch. The morning light filtered through frosted glass, illuminating her face in unforgiving clarity. Dark circles hung beneath eyes that belonged to a stranger.

"Emma?" Alex's voice carried through the closed door. "Lily's home. She's asking for you."

Her pulse quickened. "I'll be right out."

She splashed cold water on her face, attempting to wash away the remnants of another night filled with fragmented nightmares. In these dreams, she was always running toward the lighthouse, always reaching for something—or someone—just beyond her grasp.

The cold water against her skin brought a momentary clarity, like breaking through the surface after being underwater too long. Emma pressed her palms against the cool porcelain of the sink, steadying herself. The bathroom—all gleaming white tiles and chrome fixtures—felt like a pristine cell rather than a sanctuary. She studied her reflection more intently, searching for traces of the woman she must have been before. The scar tissue under her fingertips felt wrong, manufactured somehow, like evidence planted at a crime scene.

"Who were you?" she whispered to her reflection. "Who am I now?"

When she emerged from the bathroom, Alex stood waiting, his tall frame blocking the hallway. He wore the navy cashmere sweater she supposedly gave him last Christmas, his surgeon's hands clasped casually before him. Everything about him projected careful perfection, from his expertly trimmed hair to his polished loafers.

"You look beautiful," he said, reaching to tuck a strand of hair behind her ear.

Emma fought the instinct to recoil. "Thank you. Where's Lily?"

"In the kitchen with Mrs. Abernathy. She's making those chocolate chip pancakes you both love."

I hate chocolate chip pancakes, Emma thought, but smiled. "Wonderful."

Alex's hand slid around her waist, drawing her closer with practiced ease. His cologne—sandalwood and cedar—enveloped her as his lips brushed her temple. "I missed you last night," he murmured. "You were restless."

"Bad dreams." She kept her voice light, neutral.

"About the accident?" His fingers stroked small circles at the small of her back.

"I can't remember the details. Just... water. Darkness." She met his gaze, searching for any flicker of guilt, any tell that might betray him. "Alex, do you think I'll ever remember what happened that night?"

Something shifted behind his emerald eyes—a calculation so swift she might have imagined it. "The mind protects itself, Em. Some memories are better left in darkness."

His arms encircled her fully now, strong and unyielding. Emma allowed herself to be held, keeping her body carefully pliant as he pressed his lips to her neck. His touch should have felt familiar, comforting—the embrace of a husband of four years. Instead, a wave of primal fear surged through her blood.

Wrong, wrong, wrong, her body screamed. *These aren't the arms that belong around you.*

His fingers traced a deliberate path along her spine, each point of contact making her skin crawl beneath the thin fabric of her nightgown. Emma closed her eyes, pretending to savor his touch while her mind frantically cataloged the physical evidence her body was providing. The disgust rising in her throat wasn't the response of a woman being held by her beloved husband—it was her instinct trying desperately to warn her.

As Alex's hands moved across her back, pulling her closer, a flash burst behind Emma's eyes—not memory but sensation:

These same hands, pinning her wrists above her head. The weight of him, crushing. His voice, terrifyingly calm: "You know I can't let you leave, Emma. Not with what you know."

Emma gasped, jerking backward.

"What's wrong?" Alex's concern appeared genuine, his brow furrowed.

"Nothing. Just—dizzy for a moment." She forced a smile. "Let's go see Lily."

"Of course." His fingers lingered on her elbow, seemingly support-ive, but Emma felt the subtle restraint in his grip. "Take your time. Your balance has been affected since the accident."

The accident you caused? she wanted to scream. Instead, she leaned subtly into him, playing the role of a dependent wife. "I'm fine now. Just a momentary spell." Downstairs, sunlight cascaded through the wall of windows overlooking the Atlantic, painting the marble countertops in honey-gold light. The kitchen gleamed with stainless steel and polished stone, a culinary showcase that stood like an unused stage set. Mrs. Abernathy, the housekeeper Alex had hired after what he called Emma's "accident," stood at the stove flipping pancakes with the rigid precision of someone who had once served in the military or worked in a five-star restaurant. Her movements were economical, practiced, her face betraying nothing.

Lily sat perched on a stool at the island counter, small legs swinging beneath her, dark hair tumbling in waves around her heart-shaped face. She looked up as Emma entered, those familiar-unfamiliar eyes—Emma's own eyes—studying her with an intensity that made Emma's skin prickle with recognition.

"Mommy." The word hung between them, weighted with doubt, a question more than a greeting.

Emma crossed the room on unsteady legs, kneeling beside the child's stool. "Good morning, sweetheart. I missed you." The words felt simultaneously true and rehearsed, as though she were an actress who had forgotten parts of her script but remembered the emotion behind them.

Lily's small hand reached out, fingers tracing Emma's cheekbone with surprising tenderness. "Did you have bad dreams again?"

Emma felt Alex stiffen beside her. A warning. "Just a few," she answered honestly, unable to lie to this solemn-faced child. "How was Grandma's house?"

"Boring. She doesn't like when I talk about the lighthouse man." Lily's voice dropped to a whisper, her eyes darting toward Alex.

A current seemed to pass between mother and daughter in that moment. Emma saw understanding in those small, grave eyes—a silent acknowledgment that transcended her fractured memories. This child, this beautiful, watchful child, knew more than she revealed.

"The lighthouse man?" Emma asked, keeping her tone light while her heart hammered against her ribs. "Who's that, darling?"

Mrs. Abernathy cleared her throat loudly. "Pancakes are ready, Dr. Sterling."

The moment shattered. Alex guided them to the table, his hand resting on the small of Emma's back in a gesture that felt less like affection and more like ownership. Throughout breakfast, Emma watched her daughter pick at her food, answering Alex's questions with a rehearsed politeness that seemed too adult for her years.

"Mrs. Abernathy makes the best pancakes, doesn't she, Lily?" Alex cut into his stack with surgical precision, the knife slicing cleanly through the layers.

Lily nodded, pushing a chocolate chip around her plate with her fork. "Yes, Daddy."

"And did Grandma take good care of you, princess?" His voice carried an undercurrent of something Emma couldn't quite name—expectation, perhaps, or warning.

"She took me shopping." Lily's voice was carefully measured, almost adult in its controlled tone. "And we watched movies with princesses in them."

"That sounds lovely," Emma interjected, desperate to connect with her daughter beyond these scripted exchanges. "Did you have a favorite princess?"

Lily's eyes darted to her father, then back to her plate. "The mermaid one."

"The one who gives up her voice," Alex added, smiling indulgently. "Lily's always been fascinated by that story, haven't you, sweetheart? The mermaid who sacrifices everything for love."

Emma felt cold at his words, at the pointed way he looked at her as he spoke them. Was it a reminder? A threat? The pancakes turned to ash in her mouth.

"Lily drew the most wonderful pictures at Grandma's," Alex announced, retrieving a folder from the counter. "Show Mommy what you made, princess."

The drawings he spread across the table depicted sunny beaches, smiling stick figures holding hands—mother, father, child—and colorful butterflies. Nothing like the hidden lighthouse sketches Emma had discovered.

"These are beautiful," Emma said, meeting Lily's gaze and seeing the truth there.

The child's expression remained carefully blank. "Grandma helped me make pretty pictures for Daddy."

Alex beamed, smoothing Lily's hair. "My little artist."

Emma studied the drawings more carefully, noting the stiff, controlled lines, the unnatural symmetry. These weren't the spontaneous creations of a child expressing herself—they were performances, just like the polite answers and forced smiles. Whatever was happening in this house, Lily was as much a prisoner as Emma herself.

After breakfast, Alex retreated to his study for a conference call, leaving Emma and Lily alone in the sunroom. The lighthouse stood visible through the windows, its white tower stark against the blue morning sky.

Emma sat beside her daughter on the window seat, heart pounding with the risk she was taking. "Lily," she whispered, "can I tell you a secret?"

The child nodded solemnly.

"I found your special drawings. The ones in the mermaid lunchbox."

Lily's eyes widened with fear. "Daddy doesn't like those pictures."

"I know, sweetheart. But I thought they were beautiful. Especially the lighthouse keeper." Emma kept her voice gentle, steady despite her racing pulse. "Can you tell me about him?"

Lily glanced toward the doorway, then leaned closer. Her small hand curled around Emma's wrist, fingers pressing against her pulse point as if confirming her mother was real, present. The child's breath smelled of toothpaste and chocolate as she whispered, "His name is Marcus. He has a hurt face, but it's not scary. He saved you from the water once. That's what you told me." Her small fingers gripped Emma's sleeve. "He says the true stories are in the tower."

The name Marcus struck Emma like a physical blow. She had no memory of the man, yet her body responded with immediate recognition—her heart racing, a flush warming her cheeks. "When did you see him?"

"Before you got hurt. We would visit when Daddy had hospital meetings." Lily's voice dropped further, nearly inaudible. "You were happy there. You laughed. Not like when you're with Daddy."

The truth of those words struck Emma with physical force. She had no memory of those lighthouse visits, yet they resonated with something essential within her. The lighthouse in her dreams wasn't just a random symbol—it was calling her back to something real, something true.

"Lily," Emma whispered, "what did you mean yesterday when you asked if I was still pretending?"

The child's face clouded. "Daddy told me you were playing a special game. That you might forget things or act different, but I should pretend everything is normal. He said it would help you get better."

Cold dread settled in Emma's stomach. Before she could respond, Alex's voice came from the doorway.

"There are my girls."

He stood watching them, phone in hand, expression unreadable. How long had he been there? How much had he heard?

"Lily, Mrs. Abernathy needs your help picking flowers for the dinner table." His tone brooked no argument.

The child slid from the window seat, casting one last meaningful glance at Emma before obediently leaving the room. Alex crossed to Emma, sitting beside her on the cushions still warm from Lily's body. His hand found hers, fingers intertwining with practiced precision. "You look troubled, love."

Emma forced herself to return his grip. "Just trying to remember," she said. "It's frustrating having these... gaps."

"I know." His thumb traced circles on her wrist, his touch clinical despite its intimacy. "Which is why I've arranged something special for tonight. A private dinner, just the two of us. To help reconnect."

Alarm bells rang in Emma's mind. "What about Lily?"

"Mrs. Abernathy will take her to the cinema. That new animated film she's been asking about." His smile didn't reach his eyes. "It's important we have time together, Em. To rebuild what was damaged."

Emma recognized the trap forming around her. "That sounds wonderful."

"Perfect." Alex leaned forward, capturing her lips in a kiss that felt like ownership rather than affection.

His hands framed her face, thumbs pressing against her jawline with subtle force. The kiss deepened, and Emma fought against the revulsion rising within her. She matched his movements, a careful counterfeit of passion, while her mind calculated escape routes and possibilities.

As his arms encircled her, another flash exploded behind Emma's eyes:

His face, contorted with rage. Glass shattering. "Do you think I'd let him take what's mine? Everything I've built?" His fist slamming into the wall beside her head. "I can make you forget him. I can make you forget everything."

Emma broke away, gasping. The room spun around her, the lighthouse through the window seeming to pulse in time with her racing heart.

"Emma?" Alex's voice came from far away. "Another episode?"

She nodded, unable to speak through the terror closing her throat. These weren't memories—they were too vivid, too immediate. They were warnings from her subconscious, fragments of truth breaking through whatever barriers Alex had erected in her mind.

"I think you need your medication." Alex stood, his doctor persona sliding into place. "You're pale. Trembling."

"No!" Emma said, too quickly. "I mean, I'm fine. Just a momentary dizzy spell."

His eyes narrowed slightly. "Nevertheless. Your recovery requires consistency."

Before she could protest further, he left for the kitchen, returning moments later with a glass of water and a small white pill.

"Alex," Emma said, trying to sound reasonable rather than frightened, "I'm wondering if the medication might be affecting my memory recovery. Maybe we could try reducing the dosage?"

His expression softened into practiced concern. "Darling, trust me. As your doctor and your husband, I know what's best for your recovery." He pressed the pill into her palm. "This will help stabilize your neurotransmitter function. The human brain is fragile after trauma."

Emma stared at the innocuous white tablet. According to her hidden journal, this was his vehicle of control—the chemical leash that kept her compliant and confused.

With steady hands, she raised the glass to her lips, tucking the pill under her tongue while pretending to swallow. She drank the water, meeting his watchful gaze over the rim of the glass.

"Good girl," he murmured, the phrase sending ice down her spine.

When he left to take a call from the hospital, Emma spat the pill into her palm and flushed it down the powder room toilet. Her reflection in the small mirror looked back with growing resolve. Whatever happened tonight, she would face it with clear eyes and an unclouded mind.

The day unfolded with excruciating slowness. Emma moved through its hours like an actress who had forgotten half her lines, improvising and watching for cues. She helped Lily with a puzzle on the living room floor, their heads bent close together over colorful cardboard pieces.

"This one goes here," Lily whispered, fitting a section of blue sky into place. "See how the edges match?"

Emma nodded, wondering if her daughter was speaking of more than just the puzzle. "You're very good at seeing patterns, aren't you, sweetheart?"

Lily's eyes, so like her own, met Emma's with startling directness. "I remember things," she said simply. "Even when I'm supposed to forget."

Before Emma could respond, Mrs. Abernathy appeared in the doorway, announcing it was time for Lily's bath before their evening outing. As the housekeeper led Lily away, the child turned back once, her small hand forming a gesture Emma didn't recognize—a curled finger, like a breaking wave.

As evening approached, Mrs. Abernathy took Lily for their outing, the child casting a backwards glance that broke Emma's heart. *I will protect you,* she silently promised. *Whatever it takes*.

Alex prepared for their "special evening" with meticulous attention to detail. He arranged flowers—white roses, not the wildflowers Emma truly loved—and selected music from a collection labeled "Emma's Favorites." None of the selections stirred any recognition within her.

"Wear this," he said, presenting a garment bag containing a silk dress in deep emerald. "You wore it the night I proposed."

The dress fit perfectly, the color exactly matching Alex's eyes. Another detail engineered to reinforce the narrative he'd constructed. Emma allowed him to zip her into it, his fingers lingering at the nape of her neck.

"Beautiful," he murmured, his breath warm against her ear. "My perfect Emma."

The word "perfect" made her skin crawl. Not beloved, not cherished—perfect, like a specimen or an experiment that had turned out exactly as designed.

Dinner was a performance of domestic intimacy. Alex poured wine, served the meal he'd ordered from her "favorite" restaurant, and guided their conversation through carefully curated topics—avoiding anything that might contradict his version of their shared past.

"Do you remember our first date?" he asked, refilling her wine glass. "The botanical gardens? You were so passionate about marine conservation that you hardly touched your lunch."

Emma smiled, pretending to search her memory. "Tell me again. I want to hear it from you."

His eyes gleamed with satisfaction as he recounted their fictional first meeting—a charity gala for ocean conservation, their immediate connection, her supposed fascination with his research. The narrative was flawless, a love story worthy of film adaptation. It was also, Emma now knew with certainty, entirely fabricated.

She nodded at the appropriate moments, asked questions that stroked his ego, all while maintaining the fiction that she was struggling to recover these precious memories. With each lie he told, Emma's certainty grew stronger. This man was not her beloved husband. He was her jailer, and tonight she would begin planning her escape.

CHAPTER FIVE

CHAPTER 5 - UNRAVELING THREADS

Emma placed the prescription slip onto the weathered counter, avoiding eye contact with the elderly pharmacist who greeted her by name with unwarranted familiarity. Alex had insisted she needed her medication refilled immediately—the pills she'd been secretly flushing down the toilet for three days.

"Mrs. Sterling, how are you feeling?" The pharmacist's spectacles caught the light as he studied the prescription. "Dr. Sterling called ahead. Said you might be a bit... disoriented."

"I'm fine," Emma replied, the lie now practiced and smooth. "Just following doctor's orders."

She wandered through the narrow aisles while waiting, fingers trailing over bottles of sunscreen and displays of vitamins. The pharmacy felt oddly safe—public enough that Alex couldn't monitor her, mundane enough that he wouldn't suspect anything significant could happen here.

The fluorescent lights buzzed overhead like distant bees, casting a harsh glow that made her skin appear waxy and pale. Emma studied the rows of medications, each promising relief from some ailment or another. How peculiar that such small capsules could alter one's perception, change brain chemistry, reshape reality. Her fingers trembled slightly as she thought of the pills she'd been prescribed—what were they actually doing to her mind?

Her fingertips brushed against a bottle of fish oil supplements. The touch ignited something—a memory of herself, filling shopping baskets with these bottles, explaining to someone about their benefits for cognitive health. The recollection vanished as quickly as it had appeared, leaving behind only a hollow ache of loss.

"I used to know things," she whispered to herself, the words barely audible. "Real things. Scientific things."

This certainty felt like the only truth she possessed. Everything else—her marriage, her home, her supposed accident—existed in a mist of doubt, details shifting whenever she tried to examine them too closely.

"Emma Walker?"

The voice came from behind her, feminine and hesitant. Emma turned to find a slender woman with short black hair and rectangular glasses, holding a prescription bag. The woman's eyes widened with wonder, as though gazing upon a ghost.

"It is you." The woman stepped closer, her dark eyes caressing Emma's face. "They said you'd moved away after the accident. I didn't believe it, but—"

"I'm sorry," Emma interrupted, heart fluttering against her ribs. "Do we know each other?"

A shadow crossed the woman's face. "Of course you wouldn't—I'm Naomi Chen. We worked together for three years at the Coastal Marine Institute." She paused, watching Emma's reaction. "We were friends."

Emma felt a flutter of recognition, like the brush of butterfly wings against her memory. "Naomi," she repeated, the name sweet and familiar on her tongue.

The pharmacist called Emma's name, holding up a white paper bag.

"Wait," Naomi said with quiet urgency as Emma turned to go. "Please. Five minutes. The coffee shop across the street."

Emma hesitated, glancing at her watch. Alex expected her home within the hour. She could already imagine his questions, his concerned frown that never quite touched his eyes, the way he'd check her pupils while pretending to caress her face. Five minutes might cost her dearly if he became suspicious.

But this woman—this potential key to her past—stood before her with eyes that reflected the same longing Emma felt in her own heart.

"Five minutes," Emma agreed, her voice a tender whisper that carried the weight of a much deeper promise. The coffee shop wrapped around them like a warm blanket—all cramped spaces and mismatched chairs that somehow fit together perfectly, like puzzle pieces that had found their home. The rich aroma of freshly ground beans hung in the air, intoxicating and comforting all at once. Emma settled at a table by the window, watching steam rise from her cup in delicate spirals that danced and disappeared. She couldn't shake the feeling of exposure, as though at any moment Alex might appear on the sidewalk, his eyes finding hers through the glass.

"They told everyone you'd gone to California after the accident," Naomi said, her careful eyes studying Emma's face like she was memorizing it. "That you needed specialized treatment, then decided to stay. But when I saw you with Alex at the hospital fundraiser last month—"

"You saw me a month ago?" Emma interrupted, leaning forward until her elbows pressed against the worn wooden table. "Before my... recent accident?"

Naomi's brow furrowed, tiny lines forming between her eyes. "Recent accident? Emma, what are you talking about?"

Emma's hands tightened around her mug, seeking warmth, seeking stability. "I woke up in the hospital two weeks ago. Alex says I was injured on our research vessel during a storm. I have no memory of the past five years—our marriage, our daughter, nothing."

"Oh my God," Naomi whispered, her face draining of color until it matched the pale foam of her latte. "He's still doing it."

"Doing what?" Emma fought to keep her voice steady, though inside her heart hammered against her ribs.

"Controlling the narrative." Naomi glanced nervously around the café, her eyes darting to each patron before returning to Emma. "Listen to me carefully, Em. There was an accident, yes, but it was a year ago, not two weeks. And you weren't on any research vessel—you were found unconscious in your car at the bottom of the cliff road near the lighthouse."

Emma's stomach dropped like she was falling through empty space. "But Alex said—"

"Alex says a lot of things." Naomi's voice hardened, the softness evaporating. "After your accident last year, you were different. Subdued. You stopped returning calls, canceled our research plans. When I finally cornered you at the university, you acted like we were barely acquaintances."

"But we were close?" Emma asked, her voice small and desperate.

"We were partners." Naomi pulled out her phone, thumbs moving quickly across the screen. "Here."

The image showed Emma and Naomi in wetsuits, arms around each other's shoulders, standing on a research vessel. Both women beamed at the camera, the ocean stretching behind them. Emma wore her hair differently—shorter, with natural highlights—and her smile reached her eyes in a way it never did in the photos at Tidemark.

Emma stared, transfixed by the stranger who was herself. This woman radiated a confidence and vigor that felt utterly foreign now. A strange ache bloomed in her chest, sweet and painful.

"My hair," she murmured, touching her own longer locks. "It was different."

"You cut it short after you started dating Marcus," Naomi said, then bit her lip as if she'd revealed too much.

"Marcus?" Emma's pulse quickened, her skin warming despite the chill in the air. "Who is Marcus?"

Naomi hesitated, glancing toward the door. "Marcus Sterling. Alex's half-brother."

The name struck Emma like a physical blow, sending tiny electric currents across her skin. Marcus Sterling. The words awakened something hidden, something precious and forbidden.

"This was three days before your first accident," Naomi explained, redirecting her attention to the photo. "We were finishing our research on marine microbiome effects on coral regeneration. You were also working on a book."

Emma's heart fluttered. "A book?"

Naomi nodded, leaning closer until their heads nearly touched. "Not a marine biology text—a novel. A psychological thriller called 'The Drowning House.' You were obsessed with it, said it was 'pouring out of you.' It was about a neuroscientist who experiments with memory manipulation on his wife."

A chill whispered across Emma's skin, raising goosebumps along her arms.

"You told me the idea came after you discovered some troubling research files on Alex's computer," Naomi continued, her voice low and urgent. "Something about memory reconsolidation techniques being tested without proper oversight. You were going to report him to the ethics committee."

"And then I had my accident," Emma whispered.

"The timing was..." Naomi trailed off, her silence more damning than any words.

Emma's thoughts raced, each revelation clicking into place like tumblers in a lock. "Alex isn't just my husband, is he? He's my doctor. My... manipulator."

Naomi reached across the table, squeezing Emma's cold hands. Her touch felt like a lifeline. "You figured it out before, Em. You were gathering evidence. You told me you'd hidden backup copies of everything—the research documents, your manuscript—somewhere he wouldn't think to look."

"Do you have a copy of the manuscript?" Emma asked, hope rising in her chest.

Naomi shook her head, crushing that fragile hope. "You kept it on a private drive. After the accident, when Alex brought you home, all your research materials and personal notes disappeared. He claimed you'd decided to step back from academic work to focus on family."

Emma thought of the hidden letters in her studio floor, the mysterious phone calls, Lily's drawings of the lighthouse man. "Naomi, what do you know about Marcus Sterling?"

The coffee cup froze halfway to Naomi's lips. "How do you know that name?"

"I don't—not really. But my daughter mentioned a 'lighthouse man.' And I found letters... addressed to someone called 'My Ligh thouse.'"

Naomi set down her cup with deliberate care, her fingers trembling slightly. "Marcus is Alex's brother. Half-brother, actually. There was bad blood between them over their father's inheritance, but it got worse when Marcus started investigating Alex's research practices."

"Why would he investigate his own brother?"

"Because patients started reporting unusual side effects. Memory problems. Personality changes." Naomi glanced toward the window, then stiffened. "Don't turn around. He's here."

"Alex?" Emma whispered, panic rising in her chest.

"No. Marcus." Despite Naomi's warning, Emma couldn't resist looking. A tall man stood across the street, watching the café with piercing intensity. Even from this distance, she could see the jagged scar that ran from his left temple to his jaw. Unlike Alex's manicured perfection, this man had a rugged presence—weathered skin, dark hair swept back from his face, shoulders broad beneath a faded denim jacket.

"He keeps the lighthouse now," Naomi explained. "After he re-signed from maritime investigation. He promised someone he'd 'keep watching the lighthouse'—though he never explained what that meant."

Emma felt a surge of recognition that went beyond memory—a bone-deep knowing. "I need to meet him."

Naomi hesitated. "Emma, if Alex finds out—"

"I need to know the truth. Please."

After a moment's consideration, Naomi nodded and gestured toward the window. The man outside straightened, then crossed the street with purposeful strides. Emma's heartbeat accelerated with each step he took toward the café door.

When he entered, the small space seemed to contract around his presence. He moved with the careful grace of someone accustomed to navigating rough terrain, his eyes never leaving Emma's face as he approached their table. Those eyes—midnight blue, not emerald like Alex's—held a storm of emotions: shock, disbelief, and something that resembled hope.

"Emma," he said, her name emerging from his lips like a prayer.

The sound of his voice sent a jolt through her system—recognition without memory, like hearing a favorite song you've forgotten you loved.

"You don't remember me," he stated, not a question but a resigned observation.

"No," Emma admitted. "But I think I need to."

Naomi stood. "I'll give you two a moment. Marcus, remember what we discussed—don't overwhelm her."

As Naomi stepped away, Marcus took her vacant seat. His hands—strong, calloused, nothing like Alex's surgical precision—rested on the table between them. The scar on his face looked more dramatic up close, the tissue puckered and white against his tanned skin.

"How did you get it?" Emma asked, gesturing to the scar.

A humorless smile touched his lips. "Sailing accident when I was investigating a suspicious drowning. At least, that's what the report says."

"You don't believe it was an accident?"

"I believe my brother has a talent for making inconvenient situations disappear." His eyes never left her face. "Like he tried to do with you."

Emma leaned forward. "Tell me what you know. Please."

The air between them seemed to crackle with unspoken words. Marcus studied her for a long moment, as though weighing how much truth she could handle.

"We met two years ago when you came to the lighthouse to photograph marine birds for your research. You were still yourself then—brilliant, passionate, independent. You mentioned concerns about Alex's research, ethical violations you'd discovered."

"Were we..." Emma hesitated, uncertain how to phrase the question.

"Friends," he supplied, though something in his eyes suggested a deeper truth. "You trusted me. When things got worse with Alex, you started coming to the lighthouse more often. You said it was the one place where you could think clearly."

His voice softened as he spoke, wrapping around each word with a tenderness that made Emma's heart ache. There was history in his cadence, intimate knowledge in the way he described her. Not the clinical observations Alex made about her behavior or recovery, but the warm recognition of someone who had truly seen her.

"And Lily?" she asked, thinking of her daughter's drawings.

His expression softened. "You brought her sometimes. She loved climbing the lighthouse stairs, counting each step out loud." A small smile touched his lips. "She called me 'The keeper of the light' at first, but that was too many words for her, so it became 'lighthouse man.'"

Emma closed her eyes, trying to summon any fragment of memory—Lily's small hand in hers, climbing narrow spiral stairs, Marcus ahead of them, pointing out the mechanism that rotated the beam. Nothing came but an impression of safety, warmth, belonging.

"The letters," she whispered. "I found letters hidden in my studio floor. Addressed to 'My Lighthouse.' Were they—"

"To me," he confirmed, his voice rough with emotion. "You wrote them in the weeks before your accident. You were afraid Alex had started monitoring your communications. The traditional way felt safer."

"What happened between us?" Emma asked, opening her eyes to meet his gaze directly.

Marcus's fingers twitched, as though fighting the urge to reach for her. "We fell in love," he said simply. "It wasn't planned. It wasn't convenient. But it was real."

The words settled over Emma like a warm coat on a cold day, both comforting and overwhelming. She glanced at her watch, anxiety flaring. "I need to get back. Alex will be suspicious."

Marcus nodded, reaching into his pocket. He withdrew a small, smooth stone—white with veins of pale blue running through it. "You gave me this once. Said it reminded you of the lighthouse in the fog. Take it. If you need me, come to the north point at sunrise. I'm there every morning."

Emma accepted the stone, its cool surface warming quickly in her palm. "Why are you helping me? If Alex is your brother—"

"Blood doesn't always mean family." His hand moved as though to touch hers, then retreated. "Some connections run deeper than genetics or legal documents."

The intensity of his gaze made her cheeks warm. There was such certainty in his eyes—such unwavering conviction in the connection he claimed they shared. Emma felt simultaneously drawn to him and frightened by the pull he exerted on her.

The bell above the café door jangled, and Naomi returned, her expression tense. "Emma, you should go. It's getting late."

Marcus stood, his height more apparent now. "Be careful," he said quietly. "Alex will notice any change in your behavior. He's... observant."

"I will." Emma slipped the stone into her pocket, then gathered her pharmacy bag. "Thank you—both of you."

As she stepped onto the sidewalk, the late afternoon sun casting long shadows across the pavement, Emma felt simultaneous fear and exhilaration. For the first time since waking in that hospital room, she had allies—people who knew pieces of her truth.

The drive back to Tidemark was a blur of coastal scenery and racing thoughts. Emma parked in the circular driveway, the mansion looming over her like a beautiful prison. Before entering, she transferred the stone from her pocket to her bra, where Alex would never discover it. The weight of it against her skin felt like a talisman—a physical reminder that her reality extended beyond Alex's carefully constructed narrative.

She found him in the kitchen, preparing dinner with the focused intensity he brought to everything.

"There you are," he said, looking up from the cutting board where he precisely diced vegetables. "I was beginning to worry. Did you get your prescription?"

"Yes." Emma held up the pharmacy bag as evidence. "There was a line."

Alex studied her face, his surgeon's eyes missing nothing. "You look flushed. Are you feeling alright?"

"Just a bit tired," she answered, moving to the refrigerator to hide her expression. "Where's Lily?"

"Still with Mrs. Abernathy. I thought they might extend their out-ing through dinner—give us more time together." He set down his knife, moving behind her to place his hands on her shoulders. "You seem tense, Em. Did something happen in town?"

Emma forced herself to lean back against him, fighting the revul-sion that threatened to betray her. "Nothing interesting. Just errands."

His fingers moved to her neck, feeling her pulse. A doctor's touch, clinical beneath its pretense of affection. "Your heart's racing."

"Is it?" She turned in his arms, offering a smile she hoped appeared genuine. "Must be your effect on me."

The lie tasted bitter on her tongue, but Alex seemed to accept it, his expression softening into satisfaction. He believed her—or at least, he wanted to believe her. That desire, Emma realized, might be her greatest protection.

Later, as they ate dinner on the terrace overlooking the ocean, Emma watched the distant lighthouse. Its beam swept across the dark-ening water in steady rhythm, a pattern of light in the gathering dusk. Each flash seemed to call to her, promising answers if only she could reach it.

Alex followed her gaze. "Beautiful, isn't it? Though I've always thought that lighthouse an eyesore. Outdated technology in the age of GPS and satellite navigation."

"I find it comforting," Emma replied truthfully. "A constant in the darkness."

"Poetic," Alex commented, refilling her wine glass. "You always did have a romantic streak."

Emma curled her fingers around the stem of her glass, feeling the hidden stone press against her skin beneath her blouse. She said noth-ing, but in her mind, she was already planning how to reach the north point at sunrise.

CHAPTER 6 - SHATTERED BARRIERS

"You're completely relaxed now, Emma," Dr. Frost's voice came from somewhere far away. "Your mind is open, receptive. We're going to explore the spaces behind the locked doors in your memory. I want you to imagine yourself holding a key that can open any door in your mind."

Emma floated in the strange liminal space of hypnosis, neither fully present nor absent. The methodical ticking of the antique wall clock faded, replaced by the rhythmic crash of waves against rocks. Dr. Frost's voice became a distant anchor as Emma drifted deeper.

"Tell me about Alex," the therapist prompted. "Not what you've been told, but what you remember."

A new sensation gripped Emma—not the gentle floating of moments before, but a violent undertow pulling her into the depths. Resistance was futile. Her body felt impossibly heavy against the leather chair, as if the gravity in the room had doubled.

"He's shouting," Emma whispered, her voice childlike and afraid. "His face is red. We're in his laboratory at the university."

She could see it now with startling clarity—the sterile white countertops, the gleaming equipment, the wall of certificates and accolades that Alex was so proud of. The scent of antiseptic and coffee lingered in the air. Outside the lab windows, evening had fallen, campus lights glowing like distant stars.

"What is he shouting about?" Dr. Frost asked calmly.

"The files. I found the files." Emma's hands twitched on the armrests, fingers curling into the soft leather. "Patient 12B showed complete memory reconstruction following targeted erasure protocol. Subject believes implanted narrative regarding childhood pet death rather than original trauma memory."

The words tumbled from her lips exactly as they'd appeared on the screen that night—clinical, cold, damning. She'd stood frozen before Alex's computer, the blue light illuminating her horrified expression.

"What was your response to finding these files?"

"I told him it was illegal—unethical. Human trials without oversight." Emma's breathing quickened, shallow and rapid. "He said I didn't understand the significance. Said some memories are like cancer, that he was saving people from themselves."

In her mind, Emma saw Alex's face contort with a rage she'd never witnessed in their present life together. Memory-Alex slammed his palm against his desk, knocking over a framed photo of them—a snapshot from their honeymoon in Greece, her hair windswept, his arm possessively around her waist.

"Who's going to believe you?" his voice echoed in her mind, the gentle cadence she knew transformed into something harsh and unfamiliar. "A marine biologist questioning cutting-edge neuroscience? They'll think you're having a breakdown."

His words had cut through her with surgical precision. The doubt that flooded her then returned now, a phantom pain from a wound she couldn't remember receiving.

"He was so convincing," Emma murmured, her brow furrowed. "For a moment, I believed him—that maybe I was misinterpreting everything, seeing monsters where there were only shadows."

Dr. Frost's pen scratched softly against her notepad. "What changed your mind?"

"The date stamps on the files," Emma replied, the memory crystallizing as she spoke. "Experimental trials beginning three years earlier than the approved research timeline. Patient identifiers that matched names from the university's outpatient clinic. It wasn't paranoia. It was evidence."

The scene in Emma's mind shifted like water washing away a drawing in sand. She was somewhere else—standing at the base of the lighthouse, rain pelting her face, fist raised to knock on the weathered door of the keeper's cottage.

"Marcus," she whispered, the name bringing warmth that spread through her chest despite the cold rain. "You've gone to the lighthouse," Dr. Frost observed. "What happens there?"

"He opens the door. Surprised to see me so late." Emma's lips curved into a faint smile. "His hair is wet—he's just showered. There's a book open on his table—Hemingway. The Old Man and the Sea."

The memory crystallized with stunning clarity: Marcus pulling her inside, concern etched across his features as he wrapped a blanket around her shoulders. His fingers brushed against her collarbone, leaving trails of warmth that had nothing to do with the worn wool.

The cottage was spare but comfortable—bookshelves lined with nautical histories and classic literature, a collection of sea glass arranged by color on the windowsill, the lingering scent of coffee and salt air. A fire crackled in the small hearth, casting dancing shadows across the whitewashed walls.

"You're soaked through," Memory-Marcus said, his voice deep and tender. "What's happened? It's nearly midnight."

"I show him the files I found," Emma continued, her voice steadier now. "He doesn't dismiss me. He listens."

In her trance, Emma's hand rose slightly, as though reaching for something—or someone. "He touches my face, brushes away rain or tears, I'm not sure which. He says, 'I've suspected something was wrong with Alex's research for months.'"

"What made him suspicious?" Dr. Frost asked.

Emma's face tensed with concentration. "The water samples. Marcus had been tracking unusual chemical signatures in the runoff from Alex's offshore research facility. Compounds that shouldn't have been there—experimental neurotransmitter inhibitors, memory consolidation accelerants."

The memory shifted again, advancing like frames in a film. Emma and Marcus bent over documents spread across his kitchen table, their heads nearly touching. His lighthouse logbook repurposed to note dates, patient initials, correlating them with Alex's research calendar.

"We work for hours," Emma narrated. "Piecing it together. When we finish, it's nearly dawn." Her voice softened. "He makes tea. We watch the sunrise from the east window. Our hands touch reaching for sugar."

Memory-Emma felt the brush of his calloused fingers against hers, the contact sending electricity coursing up her arm. They froze, teaspoons suspended over their mugs, eyes locked in silent recognition of something neither had dared acknowledge before.

"I remember how he looked in that moment," Emma whispered, her face softening. "Tired but resolute. The sunrise painted him in amber and gold. His eyes never left mine, even as he set down his spoon."

Dr. Frost's voice seemed to come from miles away. "What happens between you and Marcus?"

Heat bloomed in Emma's cheeks. "He kisses me. Or I kiss him. I'm not sure who moves first. But once it starts, it feels like—"

"Like what, Emma?"

"Like coming home." The words emerged in a whisper. "Like finding something I've been searching for without knowing it was missing."

The memory intensified—Marcus's hands tangled in her hair, her back pressed against the rough stone wall of the cottage. The desperate intensity of that first kiss, born from shared danger and mutual recognition of something deeper than attraction.

"We don't plan it," Emma said, her voice catching. "But it happens. There on his narrow bed with the sound of waves crashing below. Afterward, he traces the freckles on my shoulder, says they're like stars in a clear night sky."

Memory-Marcus whispered against her skin, "I've watched you for so long, walking the shore with your sample cases. Brilliant and beautiful and utterly unaware of either."

"I told him I had noticed him too," Emma continued, "watching from the lighthouse, moving between sky and sea like he belonged to both. We'd exchanged pleasantries at the local market, discussed tide patterns and weather systems—always talking around what we really wanted to say."

Dr. Frost cleared her throat gently. "These memories feel very vivid. What else do you recall about your relationship with Marcus?"

"Secret meetings. Notes hidden in research papers. Walks on remote beaches where no one would see us." Emma's expression softened into something tender and raw. "I tell him I'll leave Alex. We plan how to expose the research violations without compromising patient privacy."

She recalled the way Marcus had crafted small gifts for her—a pendant made from polished sea glass, a journal bound in soft leather for her observations, a pressed wildflower from the lighthouse grounds tucked into a book he lent her.

"He understood what was at stake," Emma said. "Not just for me, but for Alex's patients, for scientific ethics. He never pushed me to act rashly, but he gave me courage to do what was right." The scene in Emma's mind changed abruptly—sunlight replaced by storm clouds, gentle intimacy by violent confrontation. Her body tensed in the therapy chair.

"We're on the water," she gasped. "Alex's research vessel. The Mnemosyne."

"Take your time," Dr. Frost encouraged. "What's happening on the boat?"

"I didn't mean to be there," Emma's words tumbled out faster. "I thought Alex was at a conference. I went to collect my research samples—evidence of the contamination from his offshore facility. But he was there, waiting."

Rain lashed the windows of Dr. Frost's office, mirroring Emma's memory with uncanny precision. Inside her mind, Emma stood on the heaving deck of the research vessel as a northeastern gale whipped the sea into foaming peaks.

"The boat was rocking violently," she continued, her knuckles white where they gripped the chair arms. "I remember the taste of salt spray, the howl of wind through the rigging. I almost turned back, but I needed those samples. We were so close to having enough evidence."

Emma recalled the moment she'd descended into the main cabin—the shock of seeing Alex seated calmly at the research station, the sample cases she needed spread open before him.

"He knows everything," Emma's voice broke. "About Marcus. About the evidence we've gathered. He has my phone—shows me texts between us. He's read everything."

Memory-Alex looked up, his face a mask of controlled fury. "Did you really think I wouldn't notice? My own wife, sneaking around with the lighthouse keeper of all people? How perfectly cliché."

"He'd been tracking my phone," Emma whispered, horror dawning anew with the memory. "Monitoring my communications, following my movements. He knew exactly what we were planning."

Emma's hands gripped the armrests tightly, knuckles whitening. "He's different—not angry like before. Cold. Calculated. He says, 'I can fix this, Emma. Fix us.'"

The memory darkened, becoming fragmented. "I try to leave. He blocks the cabin door. There's something in his hand—a syringe. He says it's his newest compound. Memory reconsolidation accelerant with targeted erasure properties."

Emma recalled the clinical detachment in Alex's eyes, as if she were merely another research subject. The storm raging outside seemed to intensify, the boat pitching violently beneath them.

"I remember screaming at him," Emma said, her voice trembling. "'You can't do this,' I told him. 'This isn't love, Alex. This is control.' But he wouldn't listen. He kept saying he was saving our marriage, saving me from my own poor judgment."

Emma's breathing became shallow, her chest rising and falling rapidly. "I fight him. Knock over equipment. The boat rocks violently in the storm. He catches my arm—says this is for the best, that he loves me too much to lose me."

She could feel it now, the bruising grip of his fingers around her wrist, the terrifying strength of desperation. Lightning flashed outside the cabin windows, illuminating his face in stark, terrible clarity.

"What happens next?" Dr. Frost prompted gently.

"Pain," Emma whispered. "In my neck. Cold spreading through my blood. His voice in my ear saying, 'When you wake up, you'll remember us correctly.' The room spins. I can't stand. Lightning strikes nearby—the brightest light I've ever seen—then darkness."

Emma fell silent, tears streaming down her face though her eyes remained closed. The weight of recovered memory pressed on her chest like a stone.

"I asked for Marcus," she said finally, her voice barely audible. "As the drug took hold, I called his name. Alex's face—God, the hatred in his eyes when I did that. He said, 'You won't even remember him when I'm done.'"

"Emma," Dr. Frost's voice was firm but gentle. "I want you to come back now. The memories will remain accessible, but the pain stays behind. When I count to five, you'll wake feeling calm and clear. One... two... three... four... five."

Emma's eyes fluttered open. The office materialized around her—tasteful furnishings in muted blues and grays, rain streaking the windows, Dr. Frost watching her with professional concern. Emma raised a trembling hand to her face, feeling the wetness on her cheeks.

"I remember," she said simply, her voice hoarse.

Dr. Frost nodded, setting aside her notebook. "Sometimes trauma creates barriers in our minds—protective walls. Your accident, which I suspect was no accident at all, combined with whatever compound Alex administered, created a particularly resilient barrier."

"But the memories were still there," Emma said wonderingly. "Waiting."

"The mind resists manipulation," Dr. Frost confirmed. "Given the right circumstances, the truth finds its way to the surface."

Emma sat up straighter, a new clarity in her eyes. "I need to see Marcus."

"I understand the impulse," Dr. Frost cautioned, "but you need to proceed with extreme care. Alex has gone to extraordinary lengths to control your perception of reality. If he suspects you've recovered these memories—"

"He'll try again," Emma finished, a chill running through her despite the office's warmth.

Dr. Frost nodded gravely. "Your situation requires both caution and courage, Emma. I can refer you to resources for domestic abuse victims, people who could help you leave safely."

"No." Emma shook her head firmly. "I can't just leave. There's Lily to consider. And Alex's patients—others he might be experimenting on without consent. I need evidence."

Dr. Frost studied her for a long moment, then sighed. "I've been practicing for twenty years. I've helped patients recover from trauma, abuse, addiction. But your case..." She hesitated. "It presents unique dangers."

"Will you help me?" Emma asked directly.

After a moment's consideration, Dr. Frost nodded once. "I'll document everything from our sessions. Create a record that could corroborate your testimony if needed." She glanced at her watch. "Our time is up for today. For your safety, I suggest we maintain the outward appearance that these are standard therapy sessions focusing on your amnesia recovery."

Emma nodded, gathering her coat and bag. At the door, she paused. "Dr. Frost? Thank you for believing me."

The therapist's expression softened momentarily. "Sometimes the most healing thing we can offer is simple validation of truth."

The rain had intensified when Emma left the building, sheets of water cascading from charcoal skies. She sat in her car, making no move to start the engine, letting the sound of rain on the roof wash over her as she processed the flood of recovered memories.

Alex had stolen her life—not just the years of memory, but her very self. Her work, her independence, her love. The man she'd believed was her devoted husband was actually her jailer, her mind his laboratory.

And Marcus—dear God, Marcus. The intensity of emotion that accompanied those recovered memories left her breathless. Not the sanitized, picture-perfect romance of Alex's fabrication, but something messy and real and powerful. The way his eyes crinkled when he laughed, the rough warmth of his hands, the safe harbor of his embrace when the world seemed to be crumbling around her.

With shaking hands, Emma started the car. For the first time since waking in that hospital room, she felt the stirrings of something beyond confusion and fear.

She felt rage.

Pure, clarifying rage that burned through the fog of doubt and confusion. Rage at the violation of her mind, the theft of her autonomy, the manipulation of her affection.

As she drove through the storm toward Tidemark, Emma knew with absolute certainty that she would reclaim her life—her true life—no matter the cost.

CHAPTER 7 - FORBIDDEN REVELATIONS

E mma's fingers trembled as she lifted the drives from their hiding place. She had searched Tidemark for days, looking for any trace of her former life, any evidence that might substantiate the memories that had returned during her session with Dr. Frost. Alex had been thorough in erasing her past—her research papers gone, her correspondence deleted, her photography archived with surgical precision to include only the narrative he wished to present.

But he had overlooked this trunk in the attic, perhaps assuming the equipment inside was merely obsolete research gear not worth destroying. Emma clutched the drives to her chest, heart racing. She glanced toward the attic stairs, listening for any sign of Alex returning early from his hospital rounds.

Silence, save for the storm.

The rain drummed against the roof in an uneven rhythm, like nervous fingers tapping on wood. Emma found the sound oddly comforting—nature's white noise masking her movements as she gathered the precious artifacts of her true past. The attic smelled of sea salt and aged wood, the particular scent of coastal homes that withstand decades of storms. Dust motes danced in the thin shafts of gray light filtering through the small dormer window.

"Please be here," she whispered to herself, the words barely audible even in the empty space. "Please give me something real."

The trunk's brass hinges had protested when she'd first opened it, a metallic groan that had sent her heart into her throat. Now, she traced her finger along the drives—small rectangles that contained the woman she had been. Someone with conviction. Someone who had loved.

Back in her studio, Emma connected the first drive to her laptop. Her marine biology research folder would provide the perfect cover should Alex check her computer. She created a subfolder labeled "Historical Reef Data" and copied the files.

Her hands moved with a precision that surprised her. This clandestine operation felt both foreign and familiar, as though her body remembered skills her mind had forgotten. A cold calculation that she suspected had served her well in her investigation before... before whatever had happened to her.

The first recording began to play, her own voice filling the room:

"August 15, 2021. Water samples from Site C show significant chemical anomalies consistent with non-native compounds. Spectrometer results inconclusive, but contamination pattern suggests regular discharge rather than accidental release. Source appears to be runoff from Sterling Neuroscience offshore facility."

Emma paused the recording, struck by the methodical determination in her own voice. She scrolled through the files—dozens of audio journals spanning months. She selected one from two months later:

"October 23, 2021. Marcus Sterling provided access to lighthouse records showing tidal patterns that support our contamination theory. The compounds appear in highest concentration during early morning hours, suggesting deliberate timing to avoid detection. Marcus has agreed to help monitor water quality and collect samples during his night shifts."

Marcus. Hearing his name in her own voice sent a wave of emotion washing over her. The name stirred something deep within—a hollow ache, a sweet pain that lingered beneath her ribs.

"Who were you to me?" she whispered to the recording, running her finger across the screen as if she might touch the past through it.

She played another file, dated November 10th. Her voice sounded different—softer, intimate. Background noise suggested waves lapping at a shore.

"Marcus brought coffee tonight. Said he couldn't sleep thinking about the samples. We watched the stars reflect on the water from the lighthouse gallery. He knows every constellation, tells stories about sailors who once navigated by them." A pause, then quieter: "His hand brushed mine when he pointed to Cassiopeia. I didn't move away."

Emma felt her cheeks warm. The woman in the recording—herself—sounded almost shy, girlish. She pressed play on the next file.

"December 1st. Marcus kissed me tonight. The lighthouse was cold, but his hands were warm. He tasted like salt and cinnamon. Said he'd been wanting to do that since the first water sample. I told him it was hardly romantic to reference toxic chemicals before a first kiss." A laugh, breathless and genuine. "He disagreed. Said anything that brought us together was the height of romance."

Emma closed her eyes, trying to summon the phantom sensation of this kiss. Nothing came, but her heart raced as if remembering for her.

More recordings followed—each revealing fragments of a relationship built during midnight research sessions and dawn sample collections. Her scientific notes increasingly interwoven with personal observations: the way Marcus's eyes crinkled when he smiled; how his voice changed when he spoke of the ocean; the precise feeling of his fingers laced through hers as they waited for test results.

In the final recording, dated just weeks before her accident, her voice trembled with urgency:

"March 18th. Marcus and I have compiled enough evidence. Sterling Neuroscience is dumping experimental compounds into the bay—chemicals nearly identical to those in their memory alteration patents. We're meeting Dr. Larch tomorrow. Marcus says this could change everything. He says..." Her voice softened. "He says afterward, when this is over, he wants to show me the lighthouse where he grew up in Maine. Says there's no better place to watch the sunrise."

The recording ended. Emma sat frozen, the weight of these revelations pressing on her chest. Not just the evidence of corporate wrongdoing—though that confirmed her suspicions about Alex and the Sterling family—but the evidence of love. Real love. The kind that made her former self's voice catch and warm when speaking a simple name.

She traced the edge of the hard drive with her fingertip. Somewhere in these files was the truth about what happened to her. And somewhere, perhaps, was Marcus himself—waiting, searching, or... something worse.

The storm intensified outside, rain lashing against the windows like tiny desperate fists. Emma quickly backed up the files to a cloud account Alex knew nothing about. Whatever happened next, she wouldn't lose these precious fragments of herself again.

Her past self had loved fiercely, investigated boldly. And that woman was still inside her, awakening with each recovered memory. November 5, 2021. First meeting with Marcus at the lighthouse to review findings. He's...not what I expected from Alex's descriptions. There's a kindness in him that his brother lacks, a genuineness. He showed me his collection of sea glass and the journals he's kept of every ship passing through the harbor for the past five years. His attention to detail may prove invaluable to our investigation.

Emma felt heat rise to her cheeks, hearing the subtle change in her tone when speaking about Marcus, even then. A warmth crept into her voice, a softening around the edges that spoke volumes more than her measured words.

The lighthouse that day stood stark against the pewter sky, a sentinel weathered by decades of salt and storm. Emma remembered the narrow spiral staircase, each step worn in the center from countless footfalls. The keeper's quarters had surprised her—not the utilitarian space she'd expected, but a room transformed by careful curation.

Glass shelves caught what little light filtered through the windows, displaying Marcus's sea glass collection: frosted whites, soft greens, rare purples, and blues that ranged from palest morning sky to the deepest midnight. Botanical sketches lined the walls, each leaf and flower rendered with scientific precision yet undeniable artistry. Navigation tools from another century gleamed on a side table—a sextant, a compass, a brass telescope.

And then there was Marcus himself. Where Alex was compact and meticulously groomed, Marcus moved with the loose-limbed ease of someone comfortable in his skin. His hair—darker than his brother's—looked perpetually windblown, and his eyes held the particular shade of the bay on clear mornings, somewhere between green and blue.

"Sorry about the clutter," he'd said, clearing books from a chair for her. His voice was deeper than Alex's, roughened slightly by salt air.

Emma noticed his hands as he showed her the sea glass—large and capable, but handling each fragile piece with unexpected gentleness. A fisherman's hands that could mend nets and haul lines, now cradling fragments of broken bottles as if they were precious gems.

"It's the broken things that become beautiful," he'd told her, holding an amber piece to catch the light. "The ocean doesn't destroy them. It transforms them."

Emma scrolled forward several weeks, hunger for these lost moments growing with each recording:

"December 12, 2021. Spent the evening reviewing research at the lighthouse. Storm came in unexpectedly—had to stay until it passed. Marcus made soup from his mother's recipe. We talked for hours about everything except Alex's research. His knowledge of marine ecosystems rivals many of my colleagues. He asked about my documentary series, said he'd watched every episode twice. The way he listens when I speak...it's like he's memorizing every word."

She closed her eyes, summoning that night from memory. The wind had howled around the lighthouse, rattling the windows. Rain lashed against the glass in horizontal sheets. Inside, the keeper's cottage had felt like the only safe place in the world.

The soup had steamed in mismatched ceramic bowls—potato and leek with fresh thyme, simple and perfect. Marcus had apologized for the dishes as he set them on the table.

"Bachelor living," he'd said with that half-smile that pulled up just one corner of his mouth. "I never saw the point in matching sets when it's usually just me."

"It has character," she'd replied, warming her hands on the bowl. "Like everything else here."

Lightning had flashed, illuminating his face in stark white light for an instant—the straight nose, the stubble along his jaw, the intensity in his eyes as he looked at her across the table.

"I've never been much of a cook," he'd admitted, a flush creeping up his neck. "But my mother always said this recipe could warm anyone on the coldest night."

Their conversation had flowed as easily as the rain down the windows. He'd asked her about the Galápagos documentary, questions that revealed he'd watched closely, noticed details even the critics had missed. They'd discussed whale migration patterns, debated climate models, shared favorite books.

When the power had failed, plunging them into darkness, Marcus had moved with the confidence of someone who knew every inch of his space. He'd lit old-fashioned oil lamps that cast soft golden circles of light, transforming the practical space into something almost magical.

"I keep these for emergencies," he'd explained, adjusting a wick. "But I've always preferred their light. There's something honest about flame."

The next recording made her breath catch:

"January 2, 2022. I can't deny it anymore. What I'm feeling for Marcus goes beyond professional collaboration or friendship. When our hands touched reaching for the same file tonight, I couldn't move, couldn't breathe. The look in his eyes told me he feels it too. This is impossible. Dangerous. I should stop seeing him, conduct our research through secure channels only. But the thought of not seeing him again feels... unbearable." Emma's pulse quickened as she selected a file from two weeks later:

"January 18, 2022. I kissed Marcus tonight. Or he kissed me. I'm not sure who moved first. We were comparing notes on Alex's research vessel schedules when a sudden silence fell between us. He touched my face with such gentleness, as if I might shatter beneath his fingertips. When our lips met, it felt like discovering something I've been searching for my entire life."

Her voice in the recording was breathless, vibrant with emotion. Emma touched her lips unconsciously, trying to recapture the feeling described.

The memory returned not just from the recording, but from her own healing mind. They'd been seated side by side at his small desk, shoulders touching as they reviewed the schedules. The night had grown late, the lighthouse beam sweeping over the water outside in its steady rhythm. One moment they were discussing the patterns they'd discovered, and the next, awareness had swept between them like an electric current, stilling their words.

Marcus had turned to her, his eyes so honest it made her chest ache. He'd raised his hand slowly, giving her every chance to pull away, and when she didn't, he'd traced her cheekbone with such tenderness that unexpected tears stung her eyes.

"Emma," he'd whispered, her name both a question and an answer.

She remembered now how she'd leaned into his touch, how she'd closed the distance between them, how his lips had met hers with a sweet hesitance that quickly deepened into something that felt like returning to a place she'd always belonged.

"What happens next will be complicated. Messy. Perhaps even dangerous. But for the first time in years, I feel fully awake. Marcus sees me—not as an extension of his life or work, but as myself. I know continuing this relationship while investigating Alex presents impossible

ethical questions, but I can't turn back now. Not from the investigation, and not from Marcus."

The recordings continued, documenting both her growing relationship with Marcus and their deepening investigation into Alex's
research. Her voice changed over the months—growing more confident, more alive. She found herself smiling as she listened to her own
happiness unfold, even as the evidence against Alex mounted.

Then came an entry that made her blood run cold:

"April 3, 2022. Found encrypted patient files on Alex's home server.
Marcus helped me break the security protocols. What we discovered
confirms our worst fears—Alex has been conducting unauthorized
memory manipulation trials on patients for years. The techniques
described are experimental and dangerous—targeted memory erasure
followed by the implantation of fabricated memories. The subjects
have no idea their minds have been altered."

Emma paused the recording, her hands trembling. She remembered
now—the horror of that discovery, sitting beside Marcus as the files
revealed the truth about her husband's work. How Marcus had placed
his hand over hers, steadying her as the implications became clear.

"We need to stop him," he'd said, his voice quiet but firm. "Whatever it takes."

The next file was dated just two days before her "accident":

"April 28, 2022. Alex knows something's changed. He's watching me constantly, questioning my research schedule, checking my
phone. I've moved the evidence to a secure location. Marcus thinks
we have enough to approach the ethics board, but I want absolute
certainty before we make accusations that will destroy Alex's career.
Despite everything, I remember the man I married—brilliant, passionate about helping patients with trauma. Something changed him,
or perhaps that man never truly existed."

She recalled the suffocating tension in those final days—Alex's scrutiny, his too-casual questions about her whereabouts, the feeling of being hunted in her own home. How she'd taken to changing her passwords daily, to checking for listening devices, to speaking guardedly even when she thought she was alone.

And through it all, Marcus had been her sanctuary—the lighthouse keeper whose steady presence guided her through the darkness.

She clicked on the final file, dated April 30, 2022—the day of the storm:

"I'm leaving Alex tonight. The evidence is overwhelming and damning. His research has crossed every ethical boundary in pursuit of memory manipulation techniques. Worst of all, I found notes suggesting he's been testing compounds on me—subtle doses in my tea when I've been 'difficult,' as he puts it. Testing my recall of carefully selected events, noting discrepancies. The realization makes me physically ill."

Emma's recorded voice grew softer, more intimate:

"Marcus has asked me to stay with him at the lighthouse cottage while we present the evidence to the authorities. Last night, he told me he loves me. Not in a grand, dramatic way, but simply, certainly, as if stating an obvious truth. 'I love you, Emma Walker,' he said, 'in a way that makes everything before you seem like practice for the real thing.'"

Emma felt tears sliding down her cheeks as her recorded self continued:

"I told him I love him too. The words felt like the truest thing I've ever said. We've agreed to move slowly once this is over, to give proper time and space to ending my marriage before beginning our life together. But I know with absolute certainty that Marcus is where I belong—where I've always belonged. Tonight, I'll meet him at the lighthouse after collecting the final evidence files from Alex's boat. By morning, this nightmare will be over, and we can begin again in the light."

The recording ended. Emma sat motionless, tears flowing freely now. The storm outside had intensified, rain lashing against the windows with renewed fury. In the distance, the lighthouse beam cut through the darkness, steady and unwavering.

But Emma had never reached the lighthouse that night. Instead, Alex had intercepted her on the research vessel, had erased her memories, had created a fiction of their perfect life together while keeping her prisoner in her own mind.

She remembered fragments now—the research vessel pitching in the storm, Alex's face transformed by rage when he discovered her downloading files, his clinical calm as he prepared the injection, explaining that she needed "treatment" for her "delusions" about his work.

"You'll thank me for this," he'd said, his voice almost gentle as the needle slid into her arm. "When you wake up, all this confusion will be gone. We'll start fresh."

And she had awakened to a new reality—one where she'd never uncovered his research, never fallen in love with Marcus, never known the truth about the man she'd married.

She ejected the drive and slipped it into her pocket along with two others containing the most damning evidence. She would need to hide them somewhere Alex would never think to look.

The inside pocket of her rain jacket, perhaps, or beneath the false bottom of her grandmother's jewelry box—a hidden compartment Alex didn't know existed.

A sudden sound from downstairs made her freeze. The front door closing. Alex's voice called up the stairs: "Emma? Are you home?"

Her heart hammered against her ribs. How much did her face reveal? Could he read the recovered memories in her eyes?

Quickly, she closed the laptop and tucked the remaining drives into a waterproof case, which she slid beneath a loose floorboard in her studio. She took a deep breath, composing her features into the placid mask she'd perfected in recent days.

"Up here," she called back, her voice steady despite the storm of emotions within. "Just doing some writing."

Heavy footsteps on the stairs. Emma's mind raced through what she had learned, what she now remembered, what she must conceal from the man who had stolen her memories.

Alex appeared in the doorway, rainwater dripping from his coat, his smile warm and seemingly genuine. "There you are. I missed you today." He crossed the room and kissed her cheek, his hands cold against her skin.

How had she never noticed before? The clinical precision of his affection, the way his eyes assessed rather than adored, the careful calculation behind each tender gesture.

"How was your session with Dr. Frost?" he asked, his eyes studying her face with the clinical attention she now recognized as assessment rather than affection.

"Good," Emma replied, forcing a smile. "We're making progress with the memory exercises."

She felt the weight of the drives in her pocket, heavy with truth. Somewhere across the harbor, the lighthouse keeper—her lighthouse keeper—was waiting for her to remember.

"I'm glad," Alex said, brushing a strand of hair from her face with calculated tenderness. "I was thinking we could have dinner at Harbor House tonight. The place where I proposed. Dr. Frost mentioned that revisiting significant locations might help trigger memories."

Emma nodded, maintaining her performance of the dutiful, recovering wife. "I'd like that."

She wondered if the proposal had even happened as she remembered it—or if that too was a fabrication, implanted to replace whatever real history they shared.

As Alex went to change, Emma turned to the window, watching the lighthouse beam sweep across the churning water. Its steady rhythm felt like a heartbeat, like a promise.

I remember you, Marcus, she thought. *And I'm coming back to you. No matter what it takes.*

The lighthouse stood sentinel against the storm, its beam cutting through rain and darkness—a beacon calling her home to the truth, to herself, to the love she had found and lost and found again in her memories.

CHAPTER 8 - SHADOWS ON THE WALL

E mma woke with the sensation of being watched. The digital clock on her nightstand read 3:17 AM—an hour when Tidemark should have been silent except for the occasional creak of century-old timbers adjusting to the coastal night air. She sat up slowly, her eyes adjusting to the darkness. The bedroom door stood ajar by several inches, though she distinctly remembered closing it before bed.

"Lily?" she whispered into the darkness. No answer came.

As she shifted to rise from bed, her foot touched something on the floor. Paper. She reached down and retrieved what appeared to be a folded drawing, carrying it to the window where the lighthouse beam provided intermittent illumination.

The drawing was done in crayon with the heavy-handed determination of a child intent on making her vision clear. Three figures stood before a crudely rendered lighthouse: a woman with long yellow hair, a tall man with a jagged red line across his face, and a smaller figure in white holding something long and thin—a blue stick or perhaps a needle. Arrows connected the figures in a triangle. The woman and the scarred man were linked by a red heart. The white-coated figure pointed his blue needle toward both of them.

Emma's hands trembled. This was the third drawing she'd found this week. Each featured the same characters in slightly different arrangements, each more unsettling than the last.

The cold floor against her bare feet sent a shiver up her spine, yet she remained frozen by the window, watching the lighthouse beam cut across the sky. It swept over the water, over the town, and then briefly, brilliantly, through her window, illuminating the drawing in her hands with stark clarity. In that flash, she noticed something she'd missed—tiny red dots scattered around the woman's head, like droplets of blood. Or perhaps they were stars.

"What are you trying to tell me, Lily?" she whispered, running her fingertip over the crayon lines. The wax felt tacky against her skin, fresh. This had been drawn tonight.

She glanced toward the bathroom, where her evening pills sat in their neat weekly organizer. Alex had been insistent about her medication regimen—"For your recovery," he'd said. "To help rebuild what was lost."

But what if they were destroying what remained?

The thought came suddenly, with such clarity that Emma nearly gasped aloud. She looked at the pills across the room, innocent in their little plastic compartments, then back at the drawing. The white-coated figure with the needle. The foggy patches in her memory that seemed to expand with each passing day.

"They're not helping me remember," she murmured to the empty room. "They're helping me forget."

Emma padded across the room to her journal—the one she kept hidden inside a hollowed-out marine biology textbook. Sitting cross-legged on the floor, she opened to her most recent entry and began to write:

May 8. Found another drawing from Lily. Same characters: me, the scarred man (Marcus?), and a doctor with a needle (Alex?). Missing time again yesterday—remembered having coffee at 10 AM, then suddenly it was 4 PM and I was in the garden with dirt under my nails. No memory of the hours between. Alex says I helped him plant tulip bulbs, but it's the wrong season for tulips. When I mentioned this, he looked startled, then laughed it off as a "charming sign" my botanical knowledge is returning.

Her handwriting grew more frantic as she continued.

But I've always known about seasons and planting times. That knowledge was never lost. What else is he lying about? And why does Lily keep drawing this scarred man? The face seems so familiar, yet when I try to focus on it, the memory slips away like water through cupped hands.

Emma flipped back through previous entries. The pattern was undeniable—increased dosages corresponded with larger gaps in her daily awareness. Sometimes hours, occasionally an entire day. Alex always had explanations that seemed plausible in the moment but fell apart under later scrutiny.

"Tuesday last week," she murmured, reading an entry. "Lost four hours. Alex said we went for a drive along the coast, but my hair wasn't windblown, and there was sand in my shoes though we supposedly never left the car."

She returned to the drawing, studying it more carefully. The lighthouse was rendered with surprising detail for a four-year-old—the spiraling staircase visible through a cutaway view, tiny windows, even the keeper's cottage attached to one side. At the bottom of the page, in the awkward printing of a child just learning to write, were the words: "Mommy's real home."

A fragment of memory flashed through her mind—the smell of salt air, rough stone walls beneath her palm, a man's voice saying her name with such tenderness it made her heart ache. Then it was gone, like breath on glass.

Emma folded the drawing and slipped it between the pages of her journal. She returned the book to its hiding place, mind racing. Lily was trying to tell her something—something important enough to risk sneaking into her bedroom in the middle of the night.

She slid back into bed, pulling the covers to her chin though the night was mild. Outside, the lighthouse beam continued its steady sweep, three flashes then darkness, three flashes then darkness. The rhythm should have been soothing, but instead, it felt like a warning, or perhaps a summons. As she drifted back to sleep, Emma could have sworn she heard footsteps retreating down the hallway—too heavy to be Lily's, too measured to be anyone who belonged in their home. Morning arrived with gray light filtering through the curtains. Emma dressed quickly, her movements automatic as she tried to organize her thoughts. She had to speak with Lily alone, away from Alex's watchful gaze.

In the kitchen, she found Alex preparing breakfast. The domestic scene would have appeared perfectly normal to an outsider—a husband making pancakes while his wife poured orange juice. But Emma now noticed the clinical precision in his movements, the way his eyes tracked her as she entered, cataloging her expressions.

"Sleep well?" he asked, his tone casual, but his attention anything but.

"Well enough," Emma replied, matching his lightness. "Is Lily up yet?"

"She's getting dressed. I laid out her clothes." Alex flipped a pancake with practiced ease. "I thought we'd visit the aquarium today. Dr. Frost mentioned it might help trigger your professional memories."

Emma nodded, swallowing her disappointment. Another supervised outing. Another day without a chance to speak freely with her daughter.

Her fingers curled around the cool glass of orange juice, squeezing until her knuckles whitened. Once, she'd been a marine biologist with a promising career studying coastal ecosystems. Now she could barely recall the Latin names of creatures she'd once cataloged with ease. The accident—the one Alex referred to but never described in detail—had apparently taken not just her memory but the very essence of her professional identity.

"Your medication is on the counter," Alex added, gesturing to the familiar pill organizer. "Don't forget."

Emma picked up the morning compartment, noticing immediately that something was different. "There are three pills here. I usually take two."

Alex didn't look up from the stove. "Dr. Frost and I discussed your progress yesterday. We're adjusting the dosage slightly—just adding a mild anti-anxiety component. You've seemed... unsettled lately."

Emma's heart raced. *He knows*. He had sensed her awakening suspicions, her recovered memories. This new pill would likely deepen the fog that already shrouded portions of her days.

She studied the additional pill—small and white with a blue band around its middle. Something about its appearance tugged at her memory. She'd seen it before, not in her pill organizer, but somewhere else. In Alex's hand, perhaps? Or in a medical textbook? The memory remained frustratingly out of reach.

"Good morning, Mommy."

Lily stood in the doorway, her small face solemn. She wore a blue dress Emma hadn't seen before, her dark hair pulled into neat braids. Her eyes—so like Emma's own—flickered meaningfully to the pills in her mother's hand.

"Good morning, sweetheart," Emma replied, making a split-second decision. She placed the pills in her mouth, reached for her orange juice, and pretended to swallow. With a sleight of hand born of desperation, she slipped the medication into her sleeve instead.

Alex turned from the stove, watching her with the attentiveness of a scientist observing an experiment. "All set?"

Emma smiled, hoping it reached her eyes. "All set."

Throughout breakfast, Emma noticed Lily watching her, the child's expression calculating beyond her years. When Alex turned to refill his coffee, Lily deliberately knocked over her milk glass, creating a distraction that allowed Emma to discreetly empty the remaining orange juice into a potted plant.

"Sorry, Daddy," Lily said, her voice small, but her eyes steady on her mother.

"It's fine, princess," Alex replied, already cleaning the spill with practiced efficiency. "Accidents happen."

Not an accident, Emma thought, meeting her daughter's gaze with new understanding. *She's helping me.*

The moment felt significant—a silent alliance forming between mother and daughter against a threat neither fully articulated but both somehow understood. It reminded Emma of something, a memory just out of reach: standing with Lily on a beach, teaching her about tide patterns, explaining how the ocean was full of secrets but would reveal them to patient observers. Had that been before the accident? It felt real, more substantial than the family photos Alex kept showing her.

After breakfast, Alex excused himself to take a phone call from the hospital. The moment he left the kitchen, Lily moved to Emma's side, pressing something into her hand—a crumpled piece of paper.

"What's this?" Emma whispered, quickly unfolding it.

"It's where the lighthouse man hides," Lily murmured, her voice barely audible. "He told me to show you when you stopped pretending."

Emma's breath caught. "Stopped pretending what, sweetheart?"

"That you don't remember him." Lily's dark eyes, so serious in her small face, held Emma's gaze. "The man with the line on his face. The one who gives you the stars."

Before Emma could question her further, Alex's footsteps approached. Lily returned to her seat, face arranged into childish innocence, while Emma tucked the paper into her pocket.

The aquarium visit proceeded like a carefully choreographed performance. Alex guided them through exhibits, providing educational commentary, his hand resting possessively at the small of Emma's back. She maintained her role—interested, grateful, slightly confused—while her mind raced with questions.

Standing before a tank of undulating jellyfish, their translucent bodies pulsing in hypnotic rhythm, Emma felt a sudden rush of familiarity. She'd been here before—not as a visitor, but as something else.

"I worked here," she said suddenly, the words escaping before she could consider them.

Alex's hand tightened slightly at her waist. "What makes you say that?"

"I just... I remember this tank. The Portuguese man-of-war exhibit. There was a problem with the filtration system." She pointed to a small access panel at the side of the tank. "We had to manually adjust the salinity levels every four hours for a week until the replacement parts arrived."

Her certainty faded under Alex's steady gaze. "That's interesting," he said carefully. "You never mentioned working at this aquarium before. Your research was primarily conducted at the university marine laboratory."

Doubt crept in, cold and insidious. Had she imagined that memory? Made it up from fragments of knowledge and desire?

"Maybe I just read about it somewhere," she conceded, though the memory of kneeling beside that panel, tools in hand, felt viscerally real.

"That's more likely," Alex agreed, his smile not quite reaching his eyes. "Your brain is still making new connections, filling in gaps. Dr. Frost calls it 'narrative bridging'—creating plausible stories to explain knowledge you have but can't place in context."

Emma nodded, letting him guide her toward the next exhibit, but a whisper of doubt remained. Why did her supposed imaginings always contradict Alex's version of her past? And why did Lily's drawings feature a scarred man Emma wasn't supposed to remember? That evening, when Alex was occupied with hospital paperwork in his study, Emma finally examined Lily's crumpled note. It contained a crude map showing what appeared to be the lighthouse and a path leading to rocks behind it. An "X" marked a specific location, with the words "Look here" written in a child's hand.

Emma traced the path with her fingertip, heart quickening. The lighthouse had featured in her dreams for months—dreams Alex had dismissed as meaningless sleep imagery. But now, holding Lily's map, she wondered if those dreams were actually memories fighting their way to the surface.

Later, as Emma helped Lily prepare for bed, she seized a moment of privacy.

"The lighthouse man," Emma whispered, tucking the blanket around her daughter. "Have you met him?"

Lily nodded solemnly. "He comes to my school sometimes. Watches me at recess. He has a sad face with a line on it." She traced a finger diagonally across her cheek. "He said to tell you he's waiting when you remember."

"Remember what, sweetheart?"

"That he's your lighthouse and you're his star." Lily's voice was matter-of-fact, as if reciting a message memorized with care.

The phrase struck Emma like a physical blow. Suddenly, she was elsewhere—standing on the lighthouse gallery, strong arms around her waist, a deep voice in her ear. *You're my star, Emma. The one constant I navigate by.*

The sensation was so vivid she could feel the cold metal railing beneath her hands, the warmth of his body against her back, the smell of salt and wool and something uniquely his. Marcus. The name came to her suddenly, with absolute certainty.

"Does Daddy know about him?" Emma asked carefully.

Lily's expression darkened. "Daddy says he's bad. But he's not bad. He gives me seashells and tells me stories about when you loved him."

"When was the last time you saw him?"

"Yesterday. At school. He said to tell you 'three more nights.'" Lily's eyelids grew heavy. "He said the medicine makes you forget, but the drawings will help you remember."

"What drawings, sweetheart?" Emma pressed gently, though she already knew.

"The ones I make for you. About the needle doctor and the light-house man and you." Lily's voice grew fainter as sleep began to claim her. "I put them where you'll find them. Under your pillow. In your books. Places Daddy doesn't look."

"What do you mean, sweetheart?"

But Lily had drifted to sleep, her breathing deep and even, small hands clutching her stuffed dolphin.

Emma lingered, studying her daughter's face. Lily had always been observant, catching things adults thought invisible to children. If she trusted this scarred man—this Marcus—perhaps Emma should trust her instincts too.

She returned to her bedroom, mind racing. She examined the pill organizer Alex had prepared for the week. Each compartment contained the standard two pills plus the new third one—white with a blue band around its middle. Carefully, she emptied each day's medication into a tissue and flushed the pills down the toilet, replacing them with similar-looking vitamins from her own supply.

That night, for the first time in months, Emma slept without chemical interference. Her dreams were vivid and disturbing—broken images of a storm at sea, the lighthouse beam slicing through rain, Marcus's face lit by lightning as he reached for her across churning water.

She woke at dawn, her mind sharper than it had been since her "accident." Without the medication dulling her senses, memories returned in quickening fragments—not in orderly progression, but in bursts of intense detail. The rough texture of Marcus's wool sweater under her fingers. The tang of salt on his lips when he kissed her after a shift watching the harbor. The way they'd stand in the lighthouse gallery, his arms around her from behind as they watched ships drift like toys on the distant horizon.

More troublingly, she remembered arguing with Alex—not as her husband, but as her colleague. They'd worked together at the marine research center, studying experimental compounds on sea life. She'd discovered something in his research methods, something that had horrified her enough to threaten exposure. After that, nothing but fragments: a storm, Marcus calling her name, then darkness and awakening to Alex telling her she was his wife, that she'd had an accident, that parts of her memory might never return.

For the next two days, Emma maintained her deception carefully. She pretended to take her medication, feigned the appropriate level of mental fogginess, and watched Alex with new clarity. She noticed how he tested her memory throughout the day—casual questions about their supposed past, subtle prompts designed to reinforce the fabricated narrative of their relationship.

Each night, another drawing appeared beneath her pillow. One showed the lighthouse with a hidden door at its base. Another depicted the doctor figure mixing something into a cup while the yellow-haired woman slept nearby.

On the third morning, Emma found not a drawing but a small blue-veined white stone—smooth from years of ocean tumbling. She recognized it instantly from her recovered memories: sea glass, Marcus's first gift to her. Alongside it lay a note in Lily's handwriting: "Tonight."

At breakfast, Alex studied her with increasing suspicion. "You seem different today," he observed, his tone casual, but his eyes sharp. "M ore... present."

Emma forced a smile. "Dr. Reynolds adjusted my medication last week. Maybe it's finally working properly."

CHAPTER 9 – POISON IN THE TEA

The idea had come to her that afternoon while Alex was performing surgery at Oceanview Medical Center. With Lily at her weekly swim lesson supervised by Mrs. Winters, the housekeeper, Emma had exactly ninety minutes alone at Tidemark. She'd spent the first ten minutes retrieving her old research laptop from beneath the loose floorboard in her studio, then another twenty minutes setting up the hidden camera application she once used for underwater documentation.

The house settled around her as she worked, its expensive silence broken only by the distant crash of waves against the cliffs below. Tidemark—a name that once evoked comfort but now felt like a prison with its gleaming surfaces and meticulously arranged furnishings. Every object seemed positioned just so, as if the entire house were a stage set rather than a home.

Emma's fingers trembled slightly as she configured the software, muscle memory guiding her through steps she hadn't performed in what felt like another lifetime. The application window displayed a perfect view of her bedroom through the tiny lens she'd disguised within her shell collection.

"Just like old times," she whispered to herself, remembering how she'd once used this same technique to document nocturnal patterns of bioluminescent marine life. Back then, she'd been tracking creatures that glowed in darkness. Now she hunted a different predator entirely.

She tested the motion sensor, ensuring it would capture anyone entering her room. The familiar work calmed her racing thoughts, giving her hands purpose while her mind cycled through possibilities. If she was wrong, the camera would record nothing but an empty room. If she was right...

The thought sent a cold ripple down her spine. She glanced at the ornate grandfather clock in the hallway—forty minutes remained before she needed to collect Lily. Just enough time to secure the camera and erase all evidence of her activities.

Emma moved through the house with deliberate care, avoiding the security cameras Alex had installed "for their protection." She knew their blind spots now, had mapped them meticulously during sleepless nights when Alex believed she was medicated into compliance.

Now, as midnight approached, she balanced the laptop on her knees, watching the live feed from her bedroom. The tiny camera was nestled among her collection of seashells on the dresser, its lens disguised as a particularly striking spiral conch. From this vantage point, it captured her bed, the doorway, and the small table where she kept her nightly tea—a special blend Alex prepared to "help with anxiety and promote restful sleep."

"Help with anxiety," Emma repeated under her breath, a bitter smile touching her lips. The words sounded hollow now, stripped of the concern that had once colored them. How easily she'd accepted his explanations in those early days after "the accident"—a term Alex used with practiced sympathy that now rang false as counterfeit coins.

Emma touched her fingers to her throat, remembering the heaviness that followed each cup, the strange dreams that came after. Not dreams—manipulated memories. She was certain of it now.

Her hiding place—a small storage closet off the main hallway—offered perfect seclusion. She'd arranged a makeshift seat among the winter blankets and rarely-used luggage, her back pressed against the wall, the laptop screen dimmed to its lowest setting. Through a crack in the door, she could see the corridor leading to her bedroom, ensuring she would have warning if Alex approached.

On screen, the bedroom door remained closed, the cup of tea cooling on the nightstand beside the rumpled bedding she'd arranged to suggest her sleeping form was buried beneath the covers. A convincing deception, she hoped, for anyone glancing in without turning on the lights.

The waiting was excruciating. Every creak of the house settling sent her heart racing. She imagined Alex discovering her empty bed, searching room by room until he found her hiding place. What would his face reveal in that moment? Concern for a confused wife? Or the cold calculation she increasingly suspected lay beneath his attentive demeanor?

The camera had been recording for three hours. Emma fast-forwarded through the empty footage, seeing only occasional sweeps of a lighthouse beam across her bedroom walls. She was beginning to wonder if her plan had failed when the doorknob turned at 12:17 AM. Emma's heart hammered against her ribs as she watched Alex enter her bedroom. He moved with the quiet confidence of someone who believed himself unobserved, carrying something small in his palm. He approached the bed, his expression softening as he gazed at what he thought was her sleeping form.

"Emma," he whispered, and the tenderness in his voice sent ice crawling down her spine.

She increased the volume, straining to catch his words as he moved to the nightstand and lifted her teacup. With practiced efficiency, he removed a small vial from his pocket and tapped white powder into her cooling tea, stirring it with his finger until it dissolved completely.

The practiced ease of his movements told its own story—this was a ritual performed countless times before. Emma watched, transfixed by the intimate horror unfolding on screen. In the cool blue glow of the laptop, Alex looked like a stranger, his familiar features transformed into something foreign by the shadows and by what she now knew.

"Just a little longer," Alex murmured, his voice barely audible over the recording. "Until you love me again. Until you forget him completely."

Emma pressed her hand against her mouth to stifle a gasp. On screen, Alex continued his nighttime ritual, apparently unaware of being recorded.

"I'm losing you again," he said to the empty bed, his voice filled with quiet desperation. "I can see it in your eyes—the same look you had before the accident. Before you tried to leave me for him."

The possessive edge in his voice made Emma's skin prickle with gooseflesh. She remembered the accident only in fragments—shattered glass, screeching tires, water rising around her. Alex had filled in the blanks, crafting a narrative of a distracted wife who'd driven off the coastal road during a storm. A tragic accident, he'd said, that had taken weeks of her memory.

He set the teacup down, then perched on the edge of the bed, reaching out to stroke what he thought was her hair beneath the covers. Emma's skin crawled at the intimate gesture.

"You're fighting the treatment," he continued. "Becoming resistant. Dr. Frost warned me this might happen." A bitter laugh escaped him. "Before I silenced her, of course."

Emma's blood turned to ice. Dr. Frost's sudden disappearance—had Alex...? She couldn't complete the thought.

The room around her seemed to shrink, the walls of the small closet pressing inward. Dr. Caroline Frost—the neurologist who had overseen what Alex called Emma's "recovery protocol." A serious woman with kind eyes who had suddenly "relocated to Switzerland for a research opportunity." Emma remembered Alex's casual explanation, how he'd brushed off her questions about saying goodbye.

"The higher dosage should help," he said, straightening the bedcovers. "This new compound is more effective at targeting episodic memory—specifically, emotional attachments. By morning, Marcus Sterling will be nothing more than a vague impression, a character from a book you once read." His voice hardened. "And this time, I'll make sure he stays that way."

Marcus Sterling. The name struck Emma like a physical blow, clearing away fog she hadn't realized surrounded her. Images flashed through her mind: a weathered face with lines that deepened when he smiled, hands calloused from rope and saltwater, the lighthouse keeper's cottage with its mismatched furniture and walls lined with nautical charts.

Alex stood, pocketing the empty vial. He moved to the dresser, adjusting the position of a framed photograph—one of their supposed wedding day. Emma remembered examining it closely the week before, noting inconsistencies in the background, wondering if it had been digitally altered.

"We were happy once," Alex said to the silent room. "Before your research took you to the lighthouse. Before my brother poisoned your mind against me. Against everything I've built." His fingers traced the frame. "You'll remember it my way soon enough."

Brother. The word hit Emma like a slap. Alex and Marcus—brothers? The revelation shifted pieces in her mind, rearranging what she thought she knew. The occasional resemblance she'd noticed between them—had she attributed it to coincidence? Or had that observation been chemically scrubbed from her consciousness?

He turned toward the door, then paused, his gaze drifting toward the collection of seashells. For a terrifying moment, Emma thought he'd noticed the camera. Her fingers hovered over the keyboard, ready to shut down the recording. But Alex merely picked up a small conch shell—not the camera—turning it over in his palm.

"You brought this back from our honeymoon in Belize," he said, replacing it carefully. "Though you probably don't remember that either."

Because it never happened, Emma thought fiercely.

The shell—she remembered collecting it, but not with Alex. It had been a brutally cold December morning, walking the tideline with Marcus, their shoulders touching as they hunched against the wind. He'd spotted it first, brushing sand from its perfect spiral before pressing it into her palm. "A treasure from the deep," he'd said, "like you."

Alex moved toward the door, his surgical precision evident in his soundless steps. Before exiting, he cast one final look at the bed. "Sweet dreams, my love. May they be the ones I've designed for you." The door closed behind him with a soft click. Emma sat frozen in the closet darkness, the recorded scene playing on repeat in her mind. She checked the time—12:23 AM. Six minutes. That's all it had taken for Alex to drug her tea and reveal his chilling intentions.

Her fingers trembled as she saved the video file, copying it to three separate drives before hiding two and keeping one in the pocket of her cardigan. Evidence. Not imagination. Not confusion. Proof that she wasn't crazy, that her suspicions about Alex weren't symptoms of trauma.

The cold logic of his actions terrified her more than any outburst could have. There was something deeply unsettling about the methodical way he administered the drugs, the clinical precision with which he was erasing her true memories and replacing them with fabrications.

With shaking hands, she loaded the second recording—footage from the previous night when she'd first set up the camera but hadn't yet created the decoy in her bed. The timestamp showed 1:42 AM. Emma watched as Alex entered her actual bedroom, approaching her genuinely sleeping form. The ritual was identical—the powder, the stirring, the whispered words. She fast-forwarded through the footage, stopping when Alex left, then continuing until—

Emma's breath caught. At 2:17 AM, the door opened again. Not Alex this time, but Lily, her small figure illuminated by the glow of a flashlight shaped like a dolphin. The child moved to Emma's bedside, carefully emptying the drugged tea into a potted plant before replacing the cup on the nightstand.

"Daddy's medicine is bad," Lily whispered to her sleeping mother. "The lighthouse man said so."

Emma pressed her fingers against her lips, tears welling in her eyes. Her daughter had been protecting her all along.

Little Lily with her serious eyes and solemn expressions—so unlike the carefree child Alex described in his stories of "before the accident." Emma had attributed the disconnect to trauma, believing Alex when he said Lily had witnessed the crash, had been frightened by her mother's changed behavior afterward.

But Lily knew. Somehow, she knew the truth.

The footage continued. Lily placed something beneath Emma's pillow—one of her drawings, no doubt—and crept back out of the room. Emma stopped the recording, her mind racing.

She remembered the drawings she'd found under her pillow over the past week—crayon sketches she'd dismissed as Lily's typical artwork. But now she recalled the recurring elements: a tower with light beams, stick figures holding hands, arrows pointing to what looked like a path through trees. Not random childish scribbles but messages. A map.

Her memories weren't false; they were being actively suppressed. Alex wasn't helping her recover; he was manipulating her consciousness, erasing the truth and replacing it with his own twisted narrative. And somehow, Lily knew. Somehow, Marcus had found a way to communicate with their daughter when he couldn't reach Emma directly.

Their daughter. The thought blazed through Emma's mind with sudden clarity. Was Lily truly Alex's child as he claimed? Or was she—could she possibly be—?

The timing aligned. Lily was five years old. Six years ago, Emma had come to Newport for her marine biology research, focusing on the impact of changing ocean temperatures on tidal ecosystems. She'd needed access to historical weather data kept at the lighthouse. She'd met Marcus Sterling. And then, according to Alex, she'd had her "accident" and lost months of memories.

Emma pulled out the blue-veined white stone from her pocket, turning it over in her palm. Sea glass, Marcus's first gift to her. The memory surfaced with painful clarity: standing on the rocky beach below the lighthouse, Marcus pressing the stone into her hand, their fingers entwining. "It reminds me of you," he'd said. "Something ordinary transformed into something precious by time and tide."

The memory felt worn smooth like the sea glass itself, as though she had revisited it countless times, holding it close during periods of confusion. A touchstone to reality when everything else seemed to shift beneath her feet.

Emma clutched the stone tightly, its edges pressing into her palm. Three more nights, Lily had said. Whatever Marcus was planning would happen soon. She needed to be ready.

The faint sound of footsteps in the hallway froze her in place. Emma held her breath as Alex passed the closet, continuing toward his study at the end of the corridor. The sounds that followed were familiar—ice clinking against glass, the soft creak of leather as he settled into his chair, the rustle of papers being sorted. His nightly routine.

Carefully, she closed the laptop and returned it to its hiding place. The hidden camera would continue recording, gathering evidence of Alex's nightly ritual. Tomorrow, she would find a way to reach the lighthouse, to follow Lily's map to the place marked with an X.

But tonight, she had to maintain her deception. With silent determination, Emma made her way back to her bedroom, careful to avoid the creaking floorboard outside Lily's room. She emptied the drugged tea into her bathroom sink, rinsed the cup, and settled into bed, leaving the lamp on as she always did.

The sheets felt different now, contaminated by knowledge of what had transpired there night after night. Emma resisted the urge to strip the bed, to burn everything Alex had touched. Instead, she arranged herself exactly as she always did, positioned so that Alex would see her from the doorway at his customary check.

Within minutes, Alex appeared in her doorway, right on schedule for his nightly check. Emma feigned drowsiness, offering him a sleepy smile.

"Still awake?" he asked, his tone concerned, loving.

"Just finishing my tea," she replied, gesturing to the empty cup. "It always helps me sleep."

The words tasted like ashes in her mouth. How many times had she spoken them, genuinely grateful for his care? The thought made her stomach clench, but she maintained her expression, keeping her eyes soft and unfocused as though already drifting toward sleep.

Alex's smile didn't reach his eyes. "That's my girl. Sleep well, Emma. Things will be clearer in the morning."

The double meaning in his words chilled her. Clearer for whom? By whose design?

"I'm sure they will," she whispered, meeting his gaze steadily.

As he turned to leave, Emma noticed something she hadn't before—a flash of deep satisfaction in his expression. The look of a man who believed himself in complete control, who had no idea his carefully constructed reality was beginning to crumble.

Emma switched off her lamp and lay in darkness, watching the lighthouse beam sweep across her ceiling. Three flashes, then darkness. Three flashes, then darkness. Like a heartbeat in the night, calling her home.

She thought of Marcus waiting, of Lily emptying drugged tea into plants, of the video evidence now hidden throughout Tidemark. For the first time since waking in that hospital room, Emma felt a surge of something powerful and unfamiliar.

Hope.

And beneath that hope, a hardening resolve. Alex had stolen her memories, her love, perhaps even years of her daughter's life. Tomorrow would bring its own challenges, but tonight, in the darkness, Emma made herself a promise: she would recover what was taken, protect what remained, and find her way back to truth—no matter what chemical barriers Alex placed in her path.

The lighthouse beam swept over her again, a steady rhythm unchanged by storms or seasons. Three flashes. A signal. A beacon.

A promise of safe harbor, waiting just beyond the treacherous waters.

CHAPTER TEN

CHAPTER 10 - SURFACING TRUTHS

T he first memory returned as Emma was brushing her teeth that morning. It struck with such force that she dropped her toothbrush, gripping the sink's edge as images flooded her consciousness.

A research vessel rocking on gentle swells. The tang of salt air. Marcus at the helm, his scarred hands confident on the wheel as they navigated toward the shoals where her monitoring equipment was anchored.

The vision was so vivid she could almost taste the salt spray on her lips, feel the gentle pitch of the deck beneath her feet. She remembered the way the sunlight had caught in Marcus's dark hair, turning the edges to gold like a halo. The warmth of his smile when he glanced back at her had once melted something inside her chest—a feeling she'd nearly forgotten.

"You okay in there?" Alex called through the bathroom door, his voice laced with what she now recognized as calculated concern.

"Fine," she replied, forcing steadiness into her tone. "Just dropped something."

Emma splashed cold water on her face, meeting her own eyes in the mirror. Behind her reflection lingered shadows of her former self—the marine biologist who had arrived at Blackwater Harbor with passion burning in her veins. The woman who had measured water samples by day and fallen in love beneath star-scattered skies. The woman who had discovered something far more dangerous than common pollution.

She traced the faint scar at her temple, hidden beneath her hairline. Had it really been from the car accident Alex described so carefully, so consistently? Or was it from that night on the cliffs, when Marcus had pulled her away from the men in dark coats, his fingers intertwined with hers as they ran?

Throughout breakfast, memories surfaced like treasures from a sunken chest—fragments of stolen kisses on the research vessel, of Marcus's calloused fingers brushing hair from her face, of whispered theories as they huddled over water samples that glowed with unnatural light. Emma tucked each recollection away, guarding them behind measured smiles.

"I've noticed you seem more alert lately," Alex remarked, studying her over his coffee cup. "The new medication adjustment must be working."

His eyes—the same deep blue that had once seemed so trustworthy—now felt like cold glass, reflecting nothing back. Watching. Always watching.

Emma nodded, maintaining eye contact despite the chill that ran down her spine. "I feel clearer," she said truthfully. "Like I'm finally breaking through the fog."

Something tender flickered in her heart—not for Alex, but for Marcus. For the truth. For the life that had been stolen from her, rewritten with clinical precision.

"Perhaps we should increase your dosage," Alex suggested, his voice light but his expression calculating. "Just to be safe."

Just to be safe. The same words he'd used since the beginning, when he'd first convinced her that her memories of Marcus were hallucinations, that the research findings were paranoid fantasies.

"Whatever you think best," Emma replied, her fingers tightening around her teacup. "You're the doctor, after all."

She watched him butter his toast with precise, measured strokes—the same hands that prepared her medication each night. Once, she had believed those hands were healing her. Now she knew they were erasing her, one carefully measured dose at a time. After Alex departed for his clinic, Emma retreated to her studio, locking the door behind her. She extracted her laptop from its hiding place and began reviewing the video evidence she'd gathered. Alex's clinical administration of the drugs, his whispered confessions to what he believed was her sleeping form, and Lily's protective intervention—they formed a constellation of truth that anchored her amid the swirling memories.

She created a timeline on blank sheets of watercolor paper, pinning them to her easel where they would appear, to any casual observer, as sketches for a new painting series. Each sheet represented a month from the past five years, marked with fragments as they returned to her.

By midmorning, Emma had filled three sheets with notes:

December, five years ago: First meeting with Marcus at the lighthouse. Historical weather data for research on changing tidal patterns. His quiet intensity. The way he listened when she spoke of her work.

The memory bloomed in vivid detail now—the exact shade of faded red in his knit cap, how he'd removed it respectfully when introducing himself. The lighthouse keeper's nephew, helping his uncle that winter. How different he was from Alex—less polished, more authentic. His hands roughened by practical work rather than sanitized by surgical gloves.

January, four years ago: Discovery of abnormal toxin levels near the offshore research platform. Sterling Neuroscience's private facility. Alex's evasive answers about their research protocols.

Emma remembered the chill that had nothing to do with the January wind as she'd stared at her test results. Compounds that shouldn't exist in nature. Synthetic neurotransmitter modulators in concerning concentrations. Alex's dismissive smile when she'd brought her findings to him. "You've misinterpreted the data, darling. Let me explain what you're actually seeing..."

February, four years ago: First kiss with Marcus during the winter storm. Power outage at the lighthouse. Candles reflecting in window glass. His hesitation—"You're my brother's wife."

Emma pressed her fingers to her lips, the sensation of that kiss returning with such clarity that her breath caught. Not fabricated. Not implanted. The emotions were too complex, too contradictory—guilt and liberation intertwined, the exhilaration of connection after months of Alex's increasing coldness.

She remembered how Marcus had stepped back, his expression tormented. How she'd been the one to move forward again, whispering, "My marriage has been over for months. Alex just hasn't admitted it yet."

Another memory surfaced, this one sharp-edged and painful:

Alex in his home laboratory, voice rising as she confronted him with water samples taken near the research platform. "You have no idea what's at stake," he'd shouted. "These compounds could revolutionize neurological treatment. A few contaminated tide pools are nothing compared to what we could accomplish."

Her own voice, steady despite her shock: "You're conducting human trials offshore to avoid oversight, aren't you? That's what those transport helicopters are for."

The shift in his expression—from anger to something more calculating. "You've always been too clever for your own good, Emma."

She shuddered, forcing herself back to the present. Outside her studio window, the ocean stretched to the horizon, sunlight fragmenting across its surface. The same ocean that had been contaminated by Alex's experiments—memory-altering compounds tested first on marine life, then on human subjects beyond regulatory reach.

Emma's hands moved almost of their own accord, selecting paints and mixing colors that matched the emotional tone of her recovering memories. She began creating a legitimate watercolor over her timeline, painting the lighthouse against a turbulent sky. The act steadied her, gave purpose to her trembling fingers as more memories crystallized.

Marcus showing her the files he'd gathered—cargo manifests, employee rotation schedules, medical supply orders too extensive for the staff listed in Sterling Neuroscience's public records.

Their growing partnership as they documented the evidence, planning to present it to the medical ethics board. The careful dance of keeping their investigation hidden from Alex while their feelings for each other deepened.

She painted thin washes of indigo and violet, building the storm clouds layer by layer, just as her memories were building. Each brushstroke brought back the texture of Marcus's woolen sweater beneath her fingers, the scent of coffee and sea salt that seemed to infuse his skin, the quiet way he'd look at her sometimes when he thought she wasn't aware.

Late nights in the lighthouse keeper's cottage, surrounded by documents, Marcus's voice soft in the lamplight: "We have enough, Emma. We can stop him."

Her response, fingers laced with his: "What happens after?"

His steady gaze: "Whatever you want to happen. I'll follow your lead."

The memory of his tenderness brought tears to Emma's eyes. Not the dramatic passion of Alex's fabricated love story, but something quieter and more powerful—a connection built on mutual respect, on seeing her fully and being seen in return. A soft knock at the studio door startled her. "Mommy? Can I come in?"

Emma quickly adjusted her painting to better conceal the timeline. "Of course, sweetheart."

Lily entered cautiously, her small face solemn. Emma recognized that expression now—not the sullenness Alex had attributed to trauma, but the careful assessment of a child forced to navigate an unstable reality.

"I made you something," Lily said, presenting a folded paper.

Emma accepted it, careful not to react when she opened it to find another map—this one more detailed than previous versions. The lighthouse, a winding path through trees, and something new: a small boat drawn at the base of the cliff below the lighthouse.

"It's beautiful," Emma said, meeting her daughter's eyes. "Thank you."

Lily glanced at the studio door, then whispered, "The lighthouse man says tomorrow night. When the moon is sleeping."

New moon. Tomorrow night would be completely dark.

"What else did the lighthouse man tell you?" Emma asked softly, kneeling to Lily's level.

Lily's expression grew more serious. "He said you're my real mommy, but sometimes you forget because Daddy gives you forgetting medicine." Her voice dropped even lower. "And he said he's going to take us home, where the sea glass comes from."

Emma's heart contracted painfully. The sea glass beach—a small cove accessible only by boat, where she and Marcus had spent countless hours collecting the ocean-smoothed treasures. Another memory Alex had attempted to erase.

She recalled how they'd shown Lily how to spot the best pieces, half-buried in the sand. How Marcus had lifted the little girl onto his shoulders to see a heron nesting in the cliffs above. The way Lily had giggled when he pretended her toes were small fish he might catch.

"Lily," she began carefully, "do you remember the lighthouse man from before? From before Mommy's accident?"

The child nodded solemnly. "He used to make pancakes shaped like starfish. And he told me stories about mermaids who could change their tails into legs." Her eyes grew wide. "Daddy says I dreamed that part up. But I didn't. It was real."

Emma pulled her daughter close, breathing in the clean scent of her hair. Another piece clicked into place—Lily's insistence on starfish-shaped pancakes every Sunday, a tradition Alex had dismissed as childish whimsy.

"I believe you," Emma whispered against Lily's hair. "And I remember too. Not everything. But more every hour."

Lily pulled back, her expression brightening. "You do? You remember the lighthouse? And—and him?"

"Yes," Emma said, the truth of it settling in her bones. "I remember."

After Lily left for her afternoon playtime with Mrs. Winters, Emma returned to her timeline, adding this new information. The pieces were forming a clear picture now: her investigation with Marcus had uncovered Alex's offshore research facility, where he was developing and testing memory reconsolidation techniques beyond ethical oversight. They had gathered evidence, planned to report him—and somewhere in that process, Emma and Marcus had fallen deeply in love.

She remembered Marcus teaching Lily to tie sailor's knots with patience no blood uncle could have surpassed. How he'd fashioned a small life jacket for her favorite teddy bear "so he can be safe on the boat too." The way he'd knelt to Lily's height when explaining things, never talking down to her.

By evening, when Alex returned from the clinic, Emma had constructed a nearly complete understanding of the past she'd lost. She greeted him with practiced normalcy, maintaining the performance of a recovering wife while the truth blazed within her like a lighthouse beam.

Over dinner, she watched him—this man she had once loved, then feared, and now faced as an adversary. He spoke of his day, of difficult surgeries and grateful patients, his manner that of a devoted husband sharing his life.

"How was your day?" he asked, refilling her water glass. "Any new memories surface?"

The question—once so concerned, now revealed as monitoring—made her skin crawl.

"Actually, yes," she said, calculating the risk of honesty. "I remembered more about my research—the coral regeneration project." A safe topic, one he would expect her to recall eventually.

Alex nodded, his expression showing just the right amount of pleased surprise. "That's wonderful, Emma. Your work was groundbreaking before the accident. Perhaps you'll return to it someday."

"Perhaps," she agreed, thinking of the research vessel she'd remembered, of Marcus at the helm. "When I'm fully recovered."

After dinner, Alex prepared her nightly tea with a performance of loving care that Emma now saw through completely. She accepted the cup with a grateful smile, waiting until he turned away before emptying it into the potted fern beside her chair.

As she performed her evening rituals—changing into nightclothes, brushing her teeth, arranging herself in bed with a book—one final memory crystallized with devastating clarity:

The night of her "accident." Racing through rain-slicked coastal roads, a bag of evidence and essential documents on the passenger seat beside her. The lighthouse beam visible through sheets of rain, guiding her toward Marcus who waited with a boat to take them to the mainland.

Headlights behind her, gaining rapidly. Alex's Jaguar, the high beams forcing her to adjust her rearview mirror. The panic as he pulled alongside, forcing her toward the guardrail. Her desperate attempt to maintain control as the car fishtailed on the wet pavement.

She remembered the sickening moment of weightlessness as the car broke through the barrier. The cold shock of water rushing in. The desperate struggle to free herself from the sinking vehicle. Then darkness.

Then Alex's voice in the hospital room days later, explaining the tragedy to concerned friends: "She was disoriented, driving too fast for the conditions. The car went through the guardrail. If those fishermen hadn't spotted the wreckage..."

Emma closed her eyes against the memory, feeling the phantom impact of the crash. Not an accident. An intercept. Alex had prevented her escape, then used her injuries as an opportunity to implement his experimental techniques—erasing her memories of Marcus, of their investigation, of her plans to leave.

"How's your book?" Alex asked from the doorway, startling her from her thoughts.

Emma looked up, forcing a tired smile. "Engaging, but I'm fading fast." She set the book aside, maintaining the illusion of drowsiness that had become routine after her nightly tea.

He approached, sitting on the edge of the bed with the careful movements of a man who believed himself to be handling delicate glass. "You seem different tonight," he observed, his eyes scanning her face. "More present."

The observation sent a bolt of fear through her, but Emma kept her expression neutral. "I feel more like myself," she said truthfully. "Like I'm finally starting to understand who I am."

Something flickered in Alex's eyes—concern, calculation, perhaps even fear. "That's all I've wanted for you," he said, reaching out to brush hair from her face. "For you to be yourself again. The woman I married."

The touch of his fingers against her skin required all her self-control not to recoil. Instead, she leaned slightly into the contact, playing her role while her mind screamed with the knowledge of his betrayal.

"I know," she whispered, meeting his gaze steadily. "And I'm getting closer every day."

Alex studied her face for a long moment, then leaned in to press a kiss to her forehead. "Sleep well, my love. Tomorrow is another day closer to having you back completely."

When he left, closing the door softly behind him, Emma released a shuddering breath. Tomorrow. The new moon. Marcus waiting with a boat below the lighthouse.

She turned to look out her window, where the lighthouse beam swept through the gathering darkness. Three flashes, then darkness. Three flashes, then darkness. A pulse of light, regular as a heartbeat. Regular as the truth.

Emma touched her fingers to the glass, watching the beam cut through the night. Within those steady flashes lived a promise—not of an idealized romance, but of something far more precious. Freedom. Truth. A life reclaimed.

Alex had stolen her past, manipulated her present, and attempted to control her future. But tomorrow night, with the moon hidden and the memories returning like tide, Emma would reclaim her life. She would take Lily and meet Marcus at the sea glass beach, leaving Alex with nothing but the empty shell of the life he had fabricated.

CHAPTER 11 – THE DROWNING HOUSE

Emma couldn't sleep. How could she, when every heartbeat brought her closer to freedom? She paced the perimeter of her bedroom, avoiding the creaky floorboards she'd mapped during her captivity. The windows were open a crack, letting in the salt-laden air that carried whispers of the sea. Outside, the darkness was nearly complete—only the distant beam of the lighthouse provided any illumination, sweeping across the rocky coastline with mechanical precision.

She paused by the windowsill, running her fingertips along the weathered wood. Five years in this room, and still it felt like a stranger's space—a beautifully appointed cell with its pale blue walls and tasteful coastal décor. The curtains stirred with the night breeze, sending shadows dancing across the hardwood floor. Each flutter seemed to whisper: tonight, tonight, tonight.

"Soon," she breathed, so softly the word barely existed.

She sat at her vanity, staring at her reflection in the dim light. The woman who gazed back was both familiar and strange—the same features she'd always known, but now animated by memories that changed everything. She touched the small scar at her temple, tracing its outline with her fingertip. The raised line of tissue was barely visible, especially when she wore her hair down as Alex preferred, but Emma knew exactly where to find it. The physical reminder of the night her love was stolen from her.

Her eyes in the mirror looked different now—alert, focused, with none of the misty confusion that had clouded them for years. The fog had lifted, bringing with it a clarity that was both terrifying and exhilarating. She leaned closer to her reflection, studying the tiny lines at the corners of her eyes, the faint shadows beneath them. Not the face of the woman in the photographs downstairs—that carefully maintained, vacant-eyed creature who smiled beside Alex at charity galas and hospital functions. This was her true face, marked by determination and the weight of recovered truths.

And then it happened. Like a dam breaking, the final missing memory crashed through her consciousness with such force that she gripped the vanity's edge to steady herself.

Rain lashing against the windshield. Wipers struggling against the deluge. Her hands white-knuckled on the steering wheel as she navigated the treacherous coastal road.

Emma closed her eyes, surrendering to the memory that had been locked away for so long.

She was in her car—the blue Subaru she'd chosen for its reliability in Blackwater Harbor's brutal winters. The passenger seat held a waterproof bag containing hard drives, laboratory notebooks, and shipping manifests—evidence of Alex's offshore research facility and unauthorized human trials.

She could smell the leather of the car seats, feel the slight vibration of the steering wheel beneath her palms. The rhythmic swish-thump of the wipers. The soft classical music she'd kept playing to calm her nerves—Bach's Cello Suite No. 1, Marcus's favorite. Details crystallized with startling clarity, as though she were reliving the moment rather than remembering it.

The dashboard clock read 11:42 PM. Marcus was waiting at the lighthouse with a boat that would take them to Portland, where they had arranged to meet with a medical ethics board investigator the following morning. Lily was already with him, bundled in warm clothes and fast asleep under the watchful eye of Marcus's uncle, the lighthouse keeper.

Emma remembered the call that had changed everything—Marcus's voice, urgent but controlled: "They're shutting down the facility. Destroying records. It's happening tonight."

His words had awakened something in her, cutting through months of careful planning and cautious evidence-gathering. There would be no perfect moment, no risk-free escape. They had to act now or lose their chance at a life together.

She'd waited until Alex was called to the hospital for an emergency procedure, then slipped into his home office. The safe behind his diplomas—opened with the combination she'd observed him using months earlier—contained the final pieces of evidence they needed: patient files documenting "memory reconditioning" experiments performed without consent.

The windshield wipers couldn't keep pace with the rain. Through the streaming glass, the lighthouse beam appeared fractured, like the broken promises between her and Alex. Yet each flash reminded her of Marcus waiting, his arms ready to hold her after so long apart, his heart beating in time with hers despite the distance.

Emma leaned forward, squinting to make out the road ahead, thinking of the warmth in Marcus's eyes when he looked at her, the gentle way he'd touch her cheek, the feel of his fingers laced with hers—stolen moments that had sustained her through the darkest nights.

That's when she noticed the headlights behind her—approaching too quickly for the treacherous conditions. Instinctively, she knew. Alex had discovered her absence, understood her intentions.

Her pulse quickened. The road ahead curved sharply, hugging the cliffside with nothing but a flimsy guardrail between the pavement and the churning ocean below. Emma accelerated, taking the curve as fast as she dared. The tires slid slightly, finding purchase at the last moment. Beyond the curve lay the lighthouse, Marcus, and everything her heart had longed for through five years of captive dreams. The pursuing vehicle closed the gap. In her rearview mirror, the high beams transformed into the familiar silhouette of Alex's Jaguar. Panic fluttered in her chest, but determination steadied her hands on the wheel. Less than a mile to the lighthouse. To Marcus. To freedom.

"Just a little further," she whispered to herself, the words a shield against the fear threatening to overwhelm her. "Just hold on."

The Jaguar pulled alongside her, forcing her toward the guardrail. Emma fought to maintain control as her right wheels edged onto the gravel shoulder. Through the passenger window, she caught a glimpse of Alex's face—not contorted with rage as she might have expected, but eerily calm. Methodical. Like he was performing a carefully planned procedure.

She remembered thinking how wrong it was—that expression. The controlled precision in his eyes as he executed what should have been an act of passion. Even in trying to kill her, Alex remained the surgeon: detached, technical, removing what he considered a problem with clinical efficiency.

"No!" Emma cried, jerking the wheel to reclaim her lane.

Too late. The Jaguar swerved sharply into her car. Metal screamed against metal. The Subaru fishtailed on the wet pavement, spinning toward the guardrail. Emma struggled with the wheel, but physics had taken control. She felt the sickening moment of impact as the car crashed through the barrier, then the weightless sensation of free fall.

Time stretched. In those suspended seconds between road and water, Emma's thoughts had crystallized with strange clarity. Not fear, not even regret, but a single, burning outrage: He cannot win. I will not let him take this from me.

Cold. That was her next coherent memory. Bitter cold as water rushed into the vehicle. The disorienting darkness as the headlights failed. The desperate struggle to unbuckle her seatbelt, to escape the rapidly sinking car.

Water roaring in her ears. The metallic taste of blood in her mouth where she'd bitten her tongue during impact. The chill that stole her breath and turned her limbs to lead. She remembered the sudden, terrible realization that she might die here—not in Alex's sterile laboratory but in the dark waters of the bay, with freedom just beyond her reach.

Emma gasped, returning to the present. Her hands trembled as she reached for her journal, recording this final memory while it remained vivid. The details matched perfectly with the physical evidence—the location of the accident, the damage to her vehicle, the injuries she'd sustained.

Not an accident. An attempted murder.

She wrote quickly, pen scratching across paper as she captured each recovered fragment. The weight of the evidence bag. The exact tone of Marcus's voice on the phone. The combination to Alex's safe: 18-24-07, Lily's birthdate in European format. Details Alex couldn't possibly have known she'd retained, small truths that had survived his chemical attempts to rewrite her memory.

She remembered surfacing, struggling to stay afloat in the churning water. The rocky shoreline had seemed impossibly distant. Her strength was failing when hands grabbed her, pulled her toward a small boat. Fishermen, she'd thought at the time. Now she wondered—had it been Alex? Had he retrieved her from the water, not to save her life, but to implement his ultimate experiment?

"The perfect subject," she murmured, recalling words from his research notes. "Tabula rasa through trauma-induced amnesia, enhanced with targeted chemical intervention."

She'd never been a patient to him—she'd been an opportunity. A chance to test his memory manipulation techniques on someone whose disappearance would raise no alarms, someone already isolated by the secrecy of their relationship. Someone whose consent he could manufacture after erasing her resistance.

Emma set down her pen, rubbing her temples. So many implications to process. Her daughter—biologically Marcus's child, not Alex's. Her research—abandoned not because of trauma, but because Alex had systematically erased her professional identity. Her marriage—a fabrication maintained through chemical manipulation and gaslighting.

The past five years unfolded in her mind with new meaning. The "medications" for her "anxiety and post-traumatic stress." The carefully controlled social interactions. The subtle reinforcement of her dependence. Alex had created the perfect environment to maintain his fiction—a remote house on the Maine coast, a small community that respected the famous doctor's privacy, a wife with "fragile mental health" who rarely ventured out unaccompanied.

She moved to the window again, drawn to the lighthouse beam like a moth to flame. Somewhere in that stone tower, Marcus watched and waited. Did he know she remembered him now? Could he sense the love that had reawakened in her heart, as unstoppable as the tide?

The thought of him sent warmth spreading through her chest—a visceral, physical reaction that Alex's concocted romance had never managed to produce. For years she'd believed her unresponsiveness was a symptom of her trauma. Now she understood it was her body's resistance to the lie. Some truths were too deeply embedded for even Alex's chemical cocktails to erase completely.

Emma pressed her palm against the cool glass. Five years of her life had been stolen. Five years of authentic connections, genuine emotions, and true memories—replaced with Alex's carefully constructed narrative. She turned away from the window, surveying the bedroom that had never truly been hers. Every inch of the space had been crafted with calculated precision—from the soft blue-gray walls to the tasteful linen curtains that framed the coastline view. The framed photographs on the dresser told a story that existed only in carefully manipulated images: Emma and Alex on their honeymoon in Santorini, laughing on a Barcelona terrace, hiking in New Zealand. Perfect moments from a marriage that was entirely fictional.

Emma ran her fingertips across the polished surface of the nightstand, studying a particularly convincing photo of them at sunset. The lighting was flawless, her smile genuine—likely taken from an actual memory with Marcus, before Alex had digitally inserted himself into the scene. The technical skill was remarkable. Chilling.

The deception extended to every corner of her life. Their wedding album downstairs contained sixty-seven professional photographs of a ceremony that never happened, featuring guests she'd never met congratulating them on their union. Each December, holiday cards arrived from "Alex's colleagues" with personal messages. Even the towels in their bathroom bore embroidered monograms of both their initials, intertwined in elegant script.

What kind of man devoted such meticulous attention to constructing a false reality? What darkness drove him to maintain this elaborate fiction for five years without a single slip-up?

A soft knock at the door froze her in place.

"Emma?" Alex's voice floated through the wood, gentle yet somehow demanding. "Are you awake?"

She glanced at the bedside clock—1:17 AM. Hours before their planned escape. Why was he up at this hour?

"Yes," she called, keeping her voice steady while sliding her journal beneath the mattress in one fluid motion. "Just having trouble sleeping."

The door opened, and Alex stood silhouetted against the hallway light. "I thought I heard you moving around," he said, his tone conveying nothing but husbandly concern. "Another headache?"

In the half-light, he appeared almost normal—sandy hair slightly mussed from sleep, wire-rimmed glasses perched on his straight nose, lips curved in a sympathetic smile. How many times had she found comfort in this exact scene? How many times had she mistaken his surveillance for care?

"Yes, just taking something for it," she lied.

Alex stepped into the room, closing the door behind him. The darkness felt suddenly oppressive, with only the distant lighthouse beam periodically sweeping through the curtains. The intermittent light transformed his features, highlighting the sharp angles of his face, the watchful intensity of his gaze.

"Let me help," he offered, moving toward her vanity where prescription bottles stood in neat rows. "The new medication works better if taken with warm liquid."

Warning signals flashed through Emma's mind. This wasn't part of their routine—an unscheduled dose, an unexpected midnight visit. Had he noticed her emptying her nightly tea? Had her questions about the past raised his suspicions?

She observed him through lowered lashes, noting the clinical precision of his movements. His fingers hovered over the collection of pill bottles, each bearing official-looking labels from his private practice. She wondered how many contained actual medication and how many held his experimental compounds.

"That's all right," she said, injecting warmth into her voice. "I've already taken something. I'm feeling better now."

Alex's hand paused above the medication. "Which one did you take?"

The question hung between them, deceptively simple yet loaded with danger. If she named the wrong medication, she would confirm his suspicions.

"The blue one," she said with careful vagueness. "The one you said works best for tension headaches."

Alex turned toward her, his face obscured by shadow. "That's right," he said after a pause that made her pulse quicken. "Good. Still, I think something warm would help. Let me make you some tea."

The subtle emphasis he placed on "tea" raised goosebumps on her arms. For years, she'd consumed his special blends without question—never wondering why they came in unlabeled containers, why he insisted on preparing them himself, why they sometimes left her disoriented or unusually compliant.

"I'll just be a moment," he said, slipping out before she could object.

When the door clicked shut, Emma stood frozen, her heart hammering against her ribs. Something was wrong. Alex never brought unplanned medication. Never disrupted their carefully established routine.

He knew. Somehow, he knew.

She moved swiftly to her closet, pulling out the small backpack she'd hidden there—packed with essentials, clothes, toiletries, and her memory journal. She added the hard drive containing video evidence of Alex tampering with her tea. Not enough for a permanent escape with Lily tonight—that plan required the new moon and Marcus's boat—but sufficient if she needed to flee temporarily.

She changed quickly from her nightgown into jeans and a thick sweater, slipping on rubber-soled boat shoes that would allow silent movement. Then she returned the backpack to its hiding spot and sat on the edge of the bed, arranging her features into a mask of drowsy compliance.

Alex returned minutes later carrying a steaming mug. "Chamomile with honey," he said, placing it on her nightstand. "Just the way you like it."

The familiar scent reached her—warm, sweet, inviting. She could almost map its components: chamomile base providing natural sedative effects, honey masking bitter medication, perhaps lavender to enhance relaxation. And underneath it all, whatever memory-altering substance he'd perfected in his offshore laboratory.

"Thank you," Emma said without reaching for the mug. "I'll drink it once it's cooled a bit."

Instead of leaving, Alex sat beside her on the bed, his weight creating a slight valley that pulled her toward him. "You know, I've been thinking," he said conversationally. "Perhaps we should get away for a while. The clinic in Switzerland has an opening next week. A change of scenery might help your recovery."

Switzerland. Far from Blackwater Harbor, the lighthouse, Marcus. Far from the evidence hidden in her studio and the investigation that had nearly killed her five years ago.

"That sounds lovely," Emma lied, mentally calculating her options. "But what about Lily's school?"

"She'll adapt," Alex dismissed. "Children are resilient. And the international exposure would be good for her."

His hand found hers, fingers intertwining with practiced familiarity. Emma forced herself not to pull away, though his touch now repulsed her. She noticed details she'd overlooked for years—how his thumb always rested precisely on her pulse point, monitoring her physical reactions. How his grip, while appearing affectionate, subtly restricted her movement.

"In fact," he continued, "I've already made preliminary arrangements. My colleague can cover my patients. We could leave as early as tomorrow evening."

Tomorrow evening. When she and Lily were supposed to meet Marcus at the lighthouse.

Emma manufactured a yawn. "It's an interesting idea," she said. "Let's discuss it in the morning when I'm more alert."

Alex's fingers tightened almost imperceptibly around hers. "Of course," he agreed. "But do drink your tea while it's still warm. You know how it helps you sleep."

CHAPTER 12 - EYE OF THE STORM

E mma stood in the doorway of Alex's home laboratory, watching him from the shadows. He worked with his back to her, unaware of her presence as he measured a clear liquid from one glass vial into another. His movements were precise, methodical—the practiced hands of a surgeon now employed in the dark art of memory manipulation.

The basement lab was Alex's sanctuary, a sterile counterpoint to the carefully decorated rooms above. Stainless steel countertops gleamed under harsh fluorescent lights. Glass cabinets displayed rows of compounds labeled in his meticulous handwriting. Computer monitors displayed brain scans and chemical formulas, the digital blueprints of his work.

The stark contrast between the warmth of their supposed home and this clinical space always unsettled Emma. This room spoke his truth—cold, calculating, controlled—while upstairs lived the lie he'd constructed for them both. The polished hardwood floors, the family photographs in handcrafted frames, the children's drawings magnetized to the refrigerator door—all carefully staged props in Alex's elaborate production.

Lightning flashed, illuminating the room in stark white for a heartbeat before plunging it back into artificial light. Emma counted silently—one, two, three—before thunder crashed overhead, rattling the glass vials. She pressed her palm against the door frame to steady herself, feeling the smooth wood grain beneath her fingertips, anchoring herself to something solid and real.

"It's beautiful, isn't it?" Alex spoke without turning. "The storm. Nature's own electrical storm matching the neurochemical ones I can create." He finally faced her, his expression unnervingly calm. "You shouldn't be down here, Emma."

A memory flashed in Emma's mind—Alex saying those exact words before, in this same room, with the same measured tone. How many times had she discovered this place? How many times had he wiped it from her mind afterward?

"Neither should you." Her voice remained steady despite the racing of her heart. "None of this should exist."

Alex tilted his head, studying her with clinical interest. His eyes—those eyes she'd once believed held love for her—scanned her face with the detached curiosity of a scientist observing an experiment. He wore the same navy sweater he'd worn at breakfast, the one she'd bought him for Christmas. Or had she? Was that another fabricated memory?

"You've stopped taking your medication," he observed, his tone more fascinated than concerned.

"I've stopped taking your lies."

Something flickered across his face—surprise, perhaps, or admiration. He set down the vial he'd been holding with deliberate care. The small clink of glass against a metal counter seemed to amplify in the tense silence.

"How long?" he asked.

"Long enough to remember." Emma stepped fully into the room, closing the door behind her with a soft click that felt somehow final. "Long enough to know that you drove me off that cliff. That you've been drugging me for five years. That Lily isn't your daughter."

The words hung between them, stripped bare of confusion or uncertainty. Emma felt a curious sense of power in naming these truths aloud, as if each syllable solidified her grip on reality.

Alex's smile was small and tight. "Memory is such a fascinating construct. So malleable, so unreliable. The human brain creates connections where none existed, fills gaps with fabrications it believes are real."

"Is that what you tell yourself?" Emma moved closer, pulling a small recording device from her pocket and placing it on the counter between them. The small red light blinked steadily, capturing every word. "That my memories of Marcus are fabrications? That the evidence I gathered against Sterling Neuroscience was imagination?"

The storm intensified outside, wind battering the small basement windows with increased ferocity. The lights flickered again, longer this time, casting momentary shadows across Alex's face that seemed to reveal something darker beneath his composed exterior.

"You don't understand what I've given you," Alex said, his voice softening. He gestured around the laboratory, his hands moving with the elegant precision that had once made him a renowned surgeon. "I've spent five years perfecting the science of memory. Do you know how many people live trapped by their worst moments? Haunted by trauma they can't escape?"

His eyes took on that passionate gleam that had once captivated her—or had she only believed it had? Emma couldn't trust any memory of their supposed relationship now, couldn't separate what might have been real from what Alex had manufactured.

"You weren't healing trauma. You were creating it," she countered, watching his expression carefully.

"I was saving us." His eyes blazed suddenly with an intensity that made Emma take a step back. "Our marriage was falling apart. You were slipping away, becoming distant, critical. I could see it happening, and nothing I did made any difference."

Emma shook her head slowly, the final pieces clicking into place. "We were never married, Alex."

The words landed between them like a physical blow. For the first time, Alex's composure truly faltered, his lips parting slightly in what might have been shock or denial.

"We could have been perfect together." He moved toward her, passionate now where he'd been controlled before. "I wasn't erasing you, Emma. I was erasing pain. Creating beautiful memories to replace painful ones. What's more loving than that?"

His voice held a note of genuine bewilderment, as if he truly couldn't comprehend why she didn't see his actions as the gift he believed them to be. The realization chilled Emma more than his anger would have.

"It wasn't love. It was possession." Lightning struck somewhere very close, the thunder immediate and deafening. The lights went out completely, plunging the laboratory into darkness before emergency generators hummed to life, bathing everything in an eerie red glow.

Emma's heart hammered against her ribcage, the sudden darkness awakening some primal fear she couldn't quite suppress.

In the crimson light, Alex's features took on a sinister cast, shadows pooling in the hollows of his cheeks, beneath his brows. He stood unnervingly still, watching her with an intensity that made her skin prickle.

"You went to him," Alex said, his voice dangerously quiet in the sudden stillness after the thunder. "My own brother. The family disappointment. The one who could never finish anything, never commit to anything. Until you."

The word "brother" triggered a cascade of recovered memories—Marcus laughing as waves crashed around his knees; Marcus reading to Lily on the porch swing; Marcus arguing fiercely with Alex in this very house, his finger jabbing toward a stack of documents.

"Marcus was investigating you." Emma's eyes adjusted to the dim red light, watching Alex's every movement. She shifted her weight slightly, preparing to move quickly if necessary. "We both were. We found the offshore facility, the unauthorized trials, the patients who disappeared after treatments went wrong."

Alex ran his hand through his perfectly styled hair, disturbing it for the first time Emma could remember. The small gesture seemed oddly human against the backdrop of his clinical precision.

"Collateral damage in service of greater progress." Alex waved his hand dismissively. "Scientific advancement requires sacrifice."

"Is that what I was? A sacrifice for your advancement?"

His expression softened in a way that might have seemed genuine once, before Emma understood the depths of his deception. "You were my greatest success." He moved to a cabinet, unlocking it with a key from his pocket. The metal scraped against metal as he turned the key with deliberate slowness. "The perfect subject. Your accident created ideal conditions—trauma-induced memory disruption that I could reshape, reinforce, rebuild. A blank canvas for my finest work."

The casual cruelty of his words struck Emma like physical blows. Not just the content, but the tone—the pride in his voice as he described violating her mind, rewriting her very self.

From the cabinet, he removed a small black case and set it on the counter, opening it to reveal a syringe and several vials. The glass gleamed dully in the red emergency lighting, the contents casting strange shadows as he lifted one to examine it.

"I don't need to erase everything," he continued, his voice taking on the soothing tone he'd used during countless "therapy" sessions. Emma recognized it now—the hypnotic cadence, the subtle modulation designed to induce compliance. "Just these new connections you're forming. These false narratives Marcus has planted."

"Stay away from me." Emma backed toward the door, her hand finding the cold metal of a laboratory stand behind her. She gripped it tight, ready to defend herself. The metal was cool against her palm, grounding her in the reality of the moment.

Alex filled the syringe with practiced efficiency, holding it up to the red light. A tiny bubble rose through the clear liquid, and he tapped it gently with his fingernail, the small sound inexplicably menacing in the tense silence.

"One treatment, Emma. Then you'll remember us correctly again."

Another lightning strike, another power surge. The regular lights flickered on for a moment, illuminating Alex's face in harsh white light—revealing a coldness, a clinical detachment that the red glow had somewhat softened. Then darkness again, leaving only the crimson emergency lights.

"There is no 'us' to remember," Emma said, gripping the metal stand tighter. The edges bit into her palm, pain clarifying her thoughts. "You manufactured everything—our wedding, our history, even photographs of places we never went together."

She remembered finding the digital manipulation software on his laptop, discovering the original photographs where Marcus had been carefully excised, replaced by Alex's image. The technical skill was impressive, the intention behind it horrifying.

Alex advanced slowly, his steps measured, unhurried. "I gave you perfect memories. Better than reality could ever be."

"You stole my reality."

"I improved it!" His voice rose with sudden fury, the mask of clinical detachment slipping. A vein pulsed at his temple, his knuckles whitened around the syringe. "I removed the mess, the disappointments, the ordinary failures of everyday life. I gave you a flawless love story!"

"No, Alex. You wrote yourself a love story and forced me to play a part in it." Emma's voice grew steadier with each word, her conviction hardening. "You didn't love me. You loved what you could make me into."

Alex's face contorted, the careful control he prided himself on fracturing before her eyes. "You have no idea what love is," he hissed. "Real love transforms. It elevates. It doesn't accept flaws—it corrects them."

The storm reached a crescendo outside, wind and rain pounding against the house with such force that the foundation seemed to tremble. Or perhaps it was just Emma, shaking with the terrible clarity of understanding exactly what Alex had done—not just to her, but to others before her.

"How many were there before me?" she asked. "How many subjects did you 'perfect'?"

Alex's smile returned, proud now. He straightened slightly, shoulders back, chin raised—a man displaying his accomplishments. "You were the culmination. The others were... practice. Refinement of technique."

"And what happened to them?"

"Some adapted beautifully. Others developed... complications."

Emma felt sick, bile rising in her throat as she pictured nameless, faceless victims. "You mean they died."

Alex shrugged slightly, the casual gesture obscene in its indifference. "The human brain is complex. Not everyone can tolerate reconditioning. But you—" His eyes softened as he gazed at her, something like genuine affection glimmering in their depths. "You were exceptional. Your mind accepted the new narratives almost eagerly."

"My mind fought you every day," Emma countered, remembering the headaches, the confusion, the moments of disconnect. "My body knew something was wrong even when my memories didn't."

She thought of the nightmares that had plagued her for years—driving off a cliff, water filling the car, a man's voice calling her name as darkness closed in. Her subconscious trying desperately to communicate what her conscious mind couldn't access.

"A temporary adjustment phase." He took another step toward her. "It will be easier this time. You've already accepted so much of what I've given you. This is just... a booster. A correction of recent deviations."

Emma's back hit the laboratory door. She reached behind her for the handle, but Alex was faster, slamming his palm against the door above her head. His body caged her, his familiar cologne—sandalwood and cedar—suddenly cloying, suffocating.

"Don't make this difficult, Emma." His voice had that doctor's cadence again—patient, authoritative. "Think of Lily. She needs stability, consistency."

The mention of Lily sent a surge of protective fury through Emma. She straightened, squaring her shoulders despite the fear thrumming through her veins. "She needs her real father."

Something dangerous flashed in Alex's eyes. "I am her father. In every way that matters."

"Marcus is her father. She knows it. She's been helping me remember."

"Impossible." But uncertainty had crept into his voice, the slightest waver betraying his doubt.

"She empties the tea you drug when you're not looking. She delivers messages. She draws pictures of the lighthouse, of the man with the scar." Emma held his gaze, watching realization dawn in his eyes. "Children see truth better than adults, Alex. She was never fooled."

Emma recalled finding Lily's hidden drawings—stick figures of a man with a jagged line across his face, a tall lighthouse, a woman with long hair swimming in blue crayon waves. The art of a child trying to communicate what she couldn't safely say aloud.

Alex's composure fractured further, his breathing becoming uneven. A fine sheen of sweat appeared on his forehead, catching the red emergency lights. "She's just a child. She believes what she's told."

"Then why does she call him 'my real daddy' in her drawings?"

The syringe trembled slightly in Alex's hand—the first imprecision in his movements Emma had ever witnessed. She pressed her advantage, stepping slightly to the side, away from being pinned against the door.

"It's over, Alex. The authorities have the evidence. Marcus has been working with federal investigators for months. They know about the offshore facility, the unauthorized trials, everything."

"You're lying." But his voice lacked conviction.

"Am I? Check your phone. The storm knocked out your security system, but I'm guessing emergency alerts are still coming through."

Alex's free hand moved to his pocket, withdrawing his phone. The screen illuminated his face as he checked it, casting blue-white light upward that transformed his expression into a mask of horror. His eyes widened, pupils dilating as he scrolled through what Emma knew would be alerts of the federal raid on Sterling Neuroscience's facilities.

"No," he whispered. "No, no, no."

In that moment of distraction, Emma acted. She brought the metal stand down hard against his arm. The syringe clattered to the floor, rolling under a cabinet. Alex howled in pain and fury, lunging toward her with hands outstretched.

Emma twisted away, putting the laboratory table between them. Glass beakers crashed to the floor as Alex swept them aside, advancing on her with a wild-eyed intensity that bore no resemblance to the controlled surgeon she had known. Shards crunched beneath his expensive leather shoes as he stalked toward her.

"You've ruined everything!" he shouted over the storm's fury. "Years of work, years of research! Do you know what we could have accomplished? Memory without pain! History without trauma! I could have given humanity the gift of perfect recall!"

"At the cost of truth," Emma countered, circling to maintain distance between them. "Without consent."

"People don't know what they need!" He slammed his fists on the table, sending more equipment crashing to the floor. A stoppered flask rolled toward Emma, leaving a trail of amber liquid that reeked of chemicals. "They cling to their pain like it's precious! They define themselves by their worst moments instead of seeing the possibility of something better!"

Another blinding flash of lightning, another immediate crash of thunder, and the main lights came back on, flooding the laboratory with harsh brightness. In the sudden illumination, Emma could see Alex clearly—disheveled, desperate, his mask of control completely shattered. His perfectly combed hair fell across his forehead; a button had torn from his shirt collar; a thin line of blood trickled from where he'd bitten his lower lip.

"I loved you," he said, his voice breaking. "Everything I did was because I loved you."

For an instant, Emma glimpsed genuine anguish in his eyes—the torment of a man whose reality was collapsing around him. Despite everything, she felt a flicker of pity.

"No, Alex. You loved the idea of me. The version you created in your own mind." Emma's voice softened with genuine sadness. "That's not love. It's obsession."

The sound of breaking glass upstairs startled them both—a window being forced open. Footsteps, voices. Alex's eyes darted to the laboratory door, then back to Emma. His expression shifted, calculation replacing desperation.

"They can't have you," he said, his voice suddenly calm again as he reached into another cabinet and withdrew a second case. "They can't have my work."

Emma recognized the look in his eyes—the same detached determination she'd glimpsed in her recovered memory of the night he'd run her off the road. The calculated precision of a man who viewed the world—and the people in it—as problems to be solved, variables to be controlled.

"Alex, don't—"

He opened the case to reveal another syringe. "One dose for you," he said quietly. "And one for me. Together in perfect memory, or together in no memory at all."

CHAPTER 13 - RACE TO THE LIGHT

E mma's lungs burned as she pushed forward against the wind, her soaked clothes clinging to her body like a second skin. The rocky path had turned treacherous with rain, slick stone threatening to send her plummeting toward the churning sea below. But her feet seemed to know this path intimately—muscle memory guiding her where artificial memories failed.

"Emma!" Alex's voice carried over the storm, closer than she'd expected. "You don't understand what you're doing!"

She didn't look back. Couldn't afford to. The lighthouse keeper's cottage lay just ahead, its weathered gray clapboards and red door exactly as she'd seen in her recurring dreams. Not dreams—memories. Real memories fighting their way back through the chemical barriers Alex had built in her mind.

The rain lashed at her face, each droplet like a tiny needle against her skin. Her breath came in ragged gasps, but still she pressed on, drawn to the cottage by something deeper than conscious thought. The narrow path curved around an outcropping of rock, revealing the full glory of the lighthouse rising stark and white against the storm-blackened sky.

Five years. He had stolen five years from her. The realization fueled her steps, lending her strength when her body wanted nothing more than to collapse.

"Emma, please!" Alex called again, his voice closer now. "You're confused! The treatment isn't complete!"

The treatment. Such a clinical word for what he'd done to her. For how he'd hollowed her out and filled the space with fabricated memories, manufactured emotions. Emma felt bile rise in her throat at the thought of his hands on her, his lips against hers, all while she believed the lie he'd constructed.

Lightning split the sky, freezing the scene in stark white brilliance. In that frozen moment, Emma saw a figure standing in the doorway of the cottage, tall and solid against the wind—Marcus.

The sight of him sent a shock through her system, a rush of feeling so powerful it made her stumble. Not the manufactured warmth Alex had tried to program into her responses to him, but something raw and real and powerful. Her heart recognized Marcus before her mind could fully process who he was.

Images flashed through her mind: Marcus's hands, rough with calluses, gentle against her skin; his laugh, deep and genuine, warming her from the inside out; his eyes, dark and knowing, seeing her—truly seeing her—in a way no one else ever had.

"Marcus," she whispered, the name like a talisman against Alex's influence.

She pushed forward with renewed determination, the cottage now less than fifty yards away. The beam from the lighthouse swept over her, then Marcus, then continued its endless rotation—connecting them briefly in its path just as they had been connected before Alex tore them apart.

"Emma!" Marcus called, his deep voice carrying even over the storm's fury. He started toward her, moving with the steady purpose of a man who would not be deterred by mere weather.

The sight of him moving toward her unlocked something else—the memory of their first meeting, right here on this storm-swept promontory. She had come to photograph the lighthouse for a travel magazine, and he had been the reluctant subject of her interview. The gruff lighthouse keeper with secrets behind his eyes. How annoyed he'd been at her questions, how steadfastly he'd refused to be photographed. And how, over the course of three rain-soaked days, they had fallen into each other's orbits, inevitable as the tides he monitored with such care.

Twenty yards now. Fifteen. Emma could see Marcus clearly—the jagged scar that ran from his jawline to his cheek, the intensity in his dark eyes, the strong hands reaching for her. Hands that had never tried to reshape her, only to hold her.

Ten yards. Five.

"Stop!" Alex's voice came from directly behind her, accompanied by the unmistakable click of a gun being cocked. Emma froze, turning slowly to face the man who had stolen five years of her life. Alex stood ten feet away, rain plastering his expensive shirt to his body, his perfectly styled hair now a sodden mess across his forehead. The gun in his hand looked wrong there—at odds with the precise surgeon's fingers that held it.

"You're not going anywhere with him," Alex said, his voice eerily calm despite the storm raging around them. "We're going inside. All of us. We're going to talk reasonably about this."

The Alex she had known—or thought she had known—during their supposed marriage had never raised his voice, never shown a hint of violence. Always reasonable, always measured, always in control. This man before her, with wild eyes and a trembling gun, was a stranger wearing a familiar face.

"There's nothing reasonable about what you've done," Emma replied, taking a deliberate step backward, closer to Marcus.

She felt Marcus move to her side, his presence warm and solid beside her. The heat of him radiated even through her rain-soaked clothes, a physical reminder of what was real in a world where her own memories couldn't be trusted.

"Put the gun down, Alex," Marcus said, his voice a low rumble that Emma felt as much as heard. "It's over. The authorities are already at the house."

Alex's eyes widened fractionally—the first crack in his composed facade. "You're lying."

"Your assistant confessed," Marcus continued, his hand finding Emma's, fingers intertwining. "Natalie couldn't live with the guilt anymore. She called me three days ago."

Emma glanced at Marcus in surprise. Natalie. The name stirred something—a kind woman with sad eyes who had administered Emma's "medication" when Alex was away. Who had sometimes looked at Emma with what she now recognized as pity.

"It's not over until I say it's over!" Alex shouted, his composure finally shattering completely. "Do you have any idea what I've created? What I've accomplished? I've mastered memory itself! I've rewritten the impossible!"

The rain seemed to intensify with his rage, sheets of water cascading around them. Emma felt Marcus's grip tighten on hers, a silent promise.

"You've tortured innocent people," Marcus countered, his voice steady. "You've played god with their minds. With Emma's mind."

Lightning flashed again, illuminating the stark lines of Alex's face—a face so similar to Marcus's, yet so different in its expression. Where Marcus's features held warmth and openness, Alex's were rigid with control, with the need to bend the world to his will.

"I gave her perfection!" Alex's hand trembled slightly, the gun wavering. "A perfect marriage. Perfect memories. A perfect life!"

Emma almost laughed at the absurdity of it. "Perfect? I lived in a fog for five years. I couldn't create—did you know that? My photography, the thing that defined me, was gone. I couldn't see the world clearly enough to capture it."

Alex dismissed this with a flick of his hand. "A necessary side effect of the treatment. Your artistic impulses were too tied to your memories of him." He jerked the gun toward Marcus. "I was working on a solution."

"You gave me a prison," Emma said quietly. "A beautiful cage is still a cage, Alex."

Rain streamed down Alex's face, mingling with what might have been tears. "Everything I did was for love."

The word hung between them, grotesque in its misapplication. Emma thought of the clinical precision with which Alex had touched her, as if following a script of how affection should be performed. How he had never really listened when she spoke, only waited for his turn to shape the conversation. How his eyes had always evaluated, never simply beheld.

"No." Emma shook her head, feeling Marcus's hand in hers, their fingers intertwining with the easy familiarity of long habit. "What you did was for control. That's not love."

The lighthouse beam swept over them again, illuminating Alex's face—the desperation there, the disbelief that his carefully constructed reality was crumbling around him.

"You don't understand what real love is," Alex insisted, taking a step forward. "It's about creating something better than the flawed reality we're given. It's about improvement. Perfection."

"You're wrong," Marcus said, his thumb brushing gently over Emma's knuckles in a gesture so natural it made her heart ache with recognition. "Real love sees the flaws and loves anyway. It doesn't try to erase them or rewrite them."

Emma felt something slot into place in her mind, a certainty that transcended Alex's chemical manipulations. "I remember now. I remember us, Marcus. Not all of it, but enough."

She turned to him, rain streaming down her face, and in his eyes she saw her own reflection—not perfect, not flawless, but whole. Known. Loved for precisely who she was.

"I remember the first time you showed me the tide pools beneath the lighthouse. How you knew the name of every creature living there. How you kissed me as the sun set and told me you'd never met anyone who saw the ocean the way you did."

The memory was vivid now—the rough texture of barnacles beneath her fingertips, the salt spray on her lips, the warmth of Marcus's hand at the small of her back as he steadied her on the slippery rocks. The way time had seemed to stop when he kissed her, the world narrowing to just the two of them amid the vastness of sea and sky.

Marcus's eyes shone with emotion. "You remembered."

"Not because of his drugs or his therapy or his manipulations," Emma said. "Because some memories are too powerful to erase. Some connections can't be broken."

"Touching," Alex snarled, the gun steadying in his hand as he aimed it directly at Marcus. "But ultimately meaningless. Memory is chemicals, electrical impulses, patterns that can be rewritten. What you're feeling now is just the result of interrupted treatment. I can fix it."

"There's nothing to fix," Emma said, rainwater running in rivulets down her neck, beneath her collar. "This is who I am. Who I've always been."

Even as she spoke, more memories surfaced—fragments of her life before Alex's intervention, pieces of herself returning like birds to roost. She remembered the small apartment above the bookshop where she'd lived, walls covered with her photographs. The cat with one bent ear that had adopted her rather than the other way around. The taste of strong black coffee at sunrise after a night of developing prints in her makeshift darkroom.

And Marcus. Always Marcus, steady as the lighthouse itself, illuminating the dark places without trying to erase them.

Lightning struck the lighthouse itself, a direct hit to the rod at its peak. The massive surge overloaded the electrical system, plunging the entire promontory into darkness for several seconds before backup generators hummed to life.

In those seconds of darkness, Alex lunged forward.

The beam from the lighthouse swept around again, revealing Alex just feet away, the gun aimed at Marcus's chest.

"Step away from her," Alex demanded. "She's my wife."

Emma felt the wrongness of those words like a physical pain. "I was never your wife," she said firmly. "The marriage certificate is forged.

The photographs are manipulated. The memories are manufactured. None of it was real."

Alex's face contorted with rage and something else—a flicker of doubt, perhaps. A momentary crack in his absolute conviction.

"It felt real," Alex insisted, his voice breaking. "It felt real to me."

For the first time, Emma saw past Alex's control to the brokenness beneath. The desperate need to shape reality rather than face it. The terror of a man who couldn't bear to see the world as it truly was.

"Because you were living in your own fantasy," Marcus said, his tone gentle despite the gun pointed at his heart. "You've been doing it for years, Alex. Ever since we were children, you've been rewriting reality to suit yourself."

Emma looked between the two men—so different yet unmistakably brothers in the set of their jaws, the shape of their brows. "He told me about your childhood, Alex. About how you would convince yourself that things happened differently than they did. How you'd insist on your version of events until everyone gave up arguing."

Alex's expression flickered with something like pain before hardening again. "He was always jealous of me," he said dismissively. "Our parents saw my potential. They knew he would never amount to anything."

"They knew you needed help," Marcus corrected gently. "They tried to get it for you. But you were always too clever, too convincing. You could always make people believe your version of reality."

The rain had begun to ease slightly, the wind less punishing. In the relative quiet, Emma could hear waves crashing against the rocks below, the rhythm as familiar to her as her own heartbeat.

"Come inside," Marcus said, nodding toward the cottage. "Put down the gun. We can talk about this."

Alex's eyes darted between them, then to the cottage door standing open behind them, warm light spilling out onto the wet stone path. Something in his expression shifted—calculation replacing rage.

"Yes," he said, his voice suddenly calmer. "Let's talk."

Emma felt Marcus tense beside her, his grip on her hand tightening slightly in warning. He didn't trust this sudden change, and neither did she. She had seen this version of Alex before—reasonable, accommodating, right before he manipulated a situation to his advantage.

"After you," Alex said, gesturing with the gun toward the cottage door.

Marcus moved first, keeping his body slightly between Emma and Alex as they backed toward the cottage. Emma felt the threshold beneath her feet as they stepped inside, the sudden warmth of the small space a stark contrast to the storm outside.

The lighthouse keeper's cottage was a single room with a sleeping loft above. A fire crackled in a small stone hearth, casting dancing shadows on whitewashed walls. Books lined rough wooden shelves. A worn leather chair sat beside the fire, a book open and face-down on its arm, as if the reader had just stepped away momentarily.

Emma felt a rush of familiarity so powerful it made her dizzy. This place. This was where she had been happy. Really, truly happy, not the manufactured contentment Alex had tried to install in her.

She remembered mornings spent curled in that chair, watching the play of light on water through the windows. Evenings with Marcus, his voice a gentle rumble as he read aloud while she sketched the ever-changing sea. The comfort of his body next to hers in the narrow bed upstairs, solid and warm in the chill coastal nights.

"Quaint," Alex said, his voice dripping with disdain as he stepped inside, closing the door behind him. "I suppose this is what passes for romance in your world. Rustic simplicity. How charming."

"It's honest," Emma replied. "There's nothing artificial here."

Alex's gaze swept the room, taking in the mismatched furniture, the shelves of books, the photographs on the mantel. He moved to examine them, keeping the gun trained on Marcus.

"Ah," he said, picking up one frame with his free hand. "The happy couple. How lovely."

Emma moved closer to see the photograph he held—herself and Marcus on the beach below the lighthouse, laughing as waves crashed around their knees. She wore a simple white dress that whipped around her legs in the wind. Marcus had his arms around her waist, looking at her with naked adoration.

"Our wedding day," Marcus said quietly. "Nothing elaborate. Just us, the lighthouse keeper as witness, and the sea."

The memory surfaced fully now—the cool sand between her toes, the salt spray in the air, the way Marcus's voice had broken slightly as he promised to love her for all his days. The simple silver band he had slipped onto her finger, worn smooth from years in his pocket while he waited for the right person to give it to.

"Not legally binding, I made sure of that," Alex said smugly. "I had all records of it erased after your 'accident.'"

"You couldn't erase what matters," Emma said, moving closer to Marcus until their shoulders touched. "The promises we made to each other."

Alex's face hardened. He set the photograph down with deliberate care, then turned to face them fully.

"Enough reminiscing. It's time to finish what we started, Emma." He reached into his pocket and withdrew a small vial and syringe—the ones he'd taken from his laboratory before chasing her. "One treatment. That's all it will take to clear these... confusions."

Emma's blood ran cold at the sight of the vial. She knew what was in it—the chemical cocktail Alex had been injecting her with for years, the solution that dissolved her real memories and left her mind soft and malleable, ready to accept whatever new reality he chose to construct.

"I'm not confused," Emma said, her voice steadier than she felt. "For the first time in five years, I see clearly."

"You think you do." Alex filled the syringe with practiced efficiency, the motion so routine he didn't need to look at what he was doing. "But that's just the effect of interrupted treatment. Your mind is creating false connections, false emotions."

"The only false emotions were the ones you manufactured," Marcus said, shifting slightly to place himself more fully between Emma and his brother.

"Stay where you are," Alex ordered, the gun and syringe creating a grotesque counterpoint in either hand. "I don't want to hurt you, Marcus. Despite everything, you're still my brother."

"Then put down the gun," Marcus said, his voice low and persuasive. "Put down the syringe. We can work through this."

"There's nothing to work through." Alex's voice had taken on that soothing, hypnotic quality Emma recognized from countless "therapy" sessions. "This is simply a medical intervention. Emma is my patient. She's experiencing a psychotic break brought on by trauma and medication irregularity."

CHAPTER 14 - SHATTERED ILLUSIONS

"One small injection," Alex said, advancing with the syringe. Its contents caught the firelight, liquid amber swirling against glass. "Then we can all start fresh."

Emma's heart hammered against her ribs, but she stood her ground. Five years of fog had given way to crystal clarity. She would not surrender to darkness again.

The cottage walls seemed to close in around them, the ancient wooden beams overhead creaking with the weight of unsaid truths. Rain lashed against the windows in rhythmic waves, like fingers tapping, demanding entry. Emma felt each droplet as if it were striking her exposed skin, awakening nerve endings long dulled by chemical sedation.

"You can't rewrite my mind anymore," she said, her voice stronger than she'd expected. "It's over, Alex."

He laughed—a soft, patronizing sound that made her skin crawl. His eyes caught the firelight, reflecting twin flames that held no warmth. "It's over when I say it's over. You're experiencing a temporary break from reality, that's all. I can fix it."

The gun remained trained on Marcus, whose muscles were coiled tight, ready to move at the slightest opportunity. His eyes never left his brother's face, searching for the boy he'd once known in the monster who stood before them. Emma saw the pain etched into Marcus's expression—pain for the brother lost long before tonight's confrontation.

"You've been 'fixing' me for five years," Emma said, taking a deliberate step backward, feeling the rough stone of the fireplace against her back. The heat seeped through her thin sweater, warming her resolve. "Erasing my life and replacing it with your fantasy."

Alex's fingers tightened around the syringe, his knuckles blanching white. "I gave you perfection!" His composure cracked, voice rising sharply in the small room. "A perfect home, a perfect marriage—"

"A perfect prison," Emma countered. "Built on lies and chemicals."

Lightning flashed outside, briefly illuminating the cottage through rain-streaked windows. In that stark, white moment, Emma caught Marcus's eye. Something passed between them—not just understanding, but a promise. His almost imperceptible nod sent a current of strength through her veins. Whatever happened next, they faced it together.

"You think what you had with him was real?" Alex gestured toward Marcus with the gun, the barrel wavering slightly with his agitation. "Some love story in this... hovel? I gave you a mansion. Respect. Status."

Emma felt a surge of pity beneath her fear. How little Alex understood about love. "You gave me emptiness," she said softly. "I felt hollow every day because somewhere inside, I knew it wasn't real."

She remembered waking beside him in that immaculate bedroom, staring at his sleeping face and feeling nothing but a vague sense of wrongness. The sensation would dissolve with the morning dose of medication, but it always returned in those vulnerable moments between sleep and waking.

Alex's face hardened, a muscle twitching beneath his eye. "It would have become real, in time. The mind adapts. Creates new patterns. The chemical interventions were just a bridge until your brain rewrote itself permanently."

"Is that what happened to your other subjects?" Marcus asked quietly. "The ones who didn't survive your 'treatments'?"

The cottage fell silent save for the persistent drumming of rain and the occasional crack of thunder. Emma watched as something flitted across Alex's face—just for an instant—before his clinical mask slipped back into place.

"Sacrifices for science. For progress," Alex replied, but his voice held a thread of defensiveness that hadn't been there before.

"For your ego," Emma corrected. She reached for Marcus's hand, their fingers intertwining with the easy familiarity of true connection. His skin was warm against hers, calloused where Alex's had always been smooth. These were hands that built things, that created rather than controlled. "You couldn't stand that I chose him. That I loved him. So you tried to erase him from my mind."

A memory resurfaced—Alex finding her in Marcus's workshop, her head thrown back in laughter as Marcus showed her a carved wooden bird, its wings caught mid-flight. The rage that had transformed Alex's handsome features into something unrecognizable. The accident that followed—that she now understood had been no accident at all.

"And I nearly succeeded," Alex said, his voice regaining that clinical detachment that had always chilled Emma to her core. He tilted his head, studying her as one might examine a mildly interesting specimen under glass. "Another month of treatment, and you wouldn't have recognized him if he'd stood right in front of you."

The fire popped and hissed, sending sparks dancing up the chimney. Outside, the storm intensified, wind howling through the eaves like a living thing.

"Do you remember the first time we met?" Emma asked suddenly, her eyes never leaving Alex's face. "At the university lecture? You were so charming, so interested in my work on memory formation."

Alex's expression softened slightly at the recollection. "You were brilliant. Your research was groundbreaking."

"And useful," Emma added. "For what you had planned."

The syringe gleamed in the firelight as Alex took another step toward Emma. "One dose. That's all it takes to reset the progress. Then we go home, and everything returns to normal."

"Normal?" Emma felt a laugh bubble up from somewhere deep inside her. It sounded foreign to her ears—when had she last truly laughed? "There's nothing normal about what you've done."

"You won't think that after the treatment," Alex promised, his voice honey-smooth. "You'll see things clearly again. The way I've designed you to see them."

"Designed," Marcus repeated, the single word laden with disgust. His grip on Emma's hand tightened. "People aren't experiments, Alex. They can't be programmed like computers."

Alex's eyes lit with that familiar academic fervor that had once so captivated Emma. "That's where you're wrong," he replied, leaning forward slightly as if giving a lecture. "The human mind is infinitely malleable. With the right chemical keys, the right suggestive programming—"

"The right torture," Emma interrupted. "The right abuse."

She remembered waking in a white room, disoriented, a needle in her arm. Alex's soothing voice telling her she'd had an accident. That she needed to rest. That he would take care of everything. The first of countless lies woven into the fabric of her reconstructed life.

Alex's expression darkened. "I've never abused you. Everything I did was for your benefit."

"Everything you did was to own me," Emma corrected. "To make me into your idea of a perfect wife."

A memory resurfaced: Alex selecting her clothes each morning, insisting she wear her hair just so, monitoring her food intake with obsessive precision. The constant corrections delivered with a smile. 'That's not quite how my Emma would phrase things.' 'My Emma prefers salmon to tuna.' 'My Emma doesn't care for abstract art.'

"And what's wrong with perfection?" Alex demanded. "What's wrong with wanting the best version of someone you love?"

"Because it wasn't me," Emma said simply. "That version of me never existed except in your mind."

The rain hammered against the cottage windows, the storm reaching new intensity. The lighthouse beam swept past again, illuminating the three of them in its cold white light before plunging the cottage back into the warm glow of firelight. Emma thought of how many times that light had passed over her as she sat in this very room with Marcus, talking into the night, their hearts opening to each other without artifice or manipulation.

"Enough talk," Alex said, advancing with newfound determination. "You'll understand once the treatment takes effect. You always do."

Marcus tensed beside Emma, preparing to intercept Alex, but she squeezed his hand in warning. Not yet. There was something she needed to do first.

"Before you inject me with that," Emma said, her voice steady despite her pounding heart, "there's something you should know."

Alex paused, curiosity momentarily overriding his urgency. "What?"

Emma reached into the pocket of her sodden jacket and withdrew a small black device. "I've been recording our entire conversation."

The device seemed to grow heavier in her palm as she held it up, a physical manifestation of all the truths Alex had tried to bury. She watched his eyes track to it, widen, then narrow with calculation.

"What?" The single word fell like a stone into the silence.

"Ever since I found my old equipment," Emma continued, gaining confidence with each word, "I've been documenting everything. Your confessions. Your threats. The details of your 'treatments.' All of it."

She remembered the moment she'd discovered her recording equipment, tucked away in a forgotten box in Marcus's workshop. How the tactile feel of the device had sparked a cascade of memories—of interviews conducted, of research meticulously documented. Of the woman she had been before Alex had rewritten her.

Alex's face underwent a series of rapid transformations—shock giving way to disbelief, then fury, then cold calculation. "Give me that," he demanded, extending his free hand.

"It's already transmitting to an external server," Emma lied smoothly. "Naomi has access. If anything happens to me, if I suddenly 'forget' again, the recording goes to the authorities."

"You're bluffing," Alex said, but doubt had crept into his voice, weakening its edges.

"Am I?" Emma held his gaze without flinching. "You've spent five years erasing me, Alex. But you never really knew me to begin with. You never bothered to learn who I really was."

The fire crackled in the grate, throwing shifting shadows across the whitewashed walls. Emma felt Marcus's presence beside her, solid and reassuring. She drew strength from him without taking her eyes off Alex.

"I know everything about you," Alex insisted, desperation threading through his words. "Every detail of your life, your preferences, your habits—"

"You know what you put there," Marcus interjected. "Not who she actually is."

Alex's expression hardened, his gaze shifting between them. The gun in his hand trembled slightly. "It doesn't matter. I can make you forget this conversation too. Reset everything."

"You can try," Emma said, her thumb pressing a button on the recording device. A small red light blinked to life, casting a crimson glow across her fingertips. "But how many times can you reset someone before there's nothing left to recover? How many of your subjects burned out that way, Alex? Their minds finally rejecting your artificial reality?"

The wind picked up outside, slamming a loose shutter against the cottage wall. The sound made Alex flinch, a hairline crack in his carefully constructed composure.

"That won't happen to you. Your brain chemistry is ideal for the treatment. I've calculated every variable," he insisted, but the tremor in his hand had worsened.

"Have you calculated what happens when federal agents raid your facilities? When they find your research notes, your chemical compounds, your list of victims?" Emma took a step forward, emboldened by the flicker of uncertainty in Alex's eyes. "Have you calculated what happens when the world discovers what you've been doing?"

She was close enough now to smell his cologne—the same scent he'd worn for years, selected because she had once, in passing, mentioned liking it. Another piece of her life he had seized upon and twisted to his purpose.

"No one will believe you," Alex said, but his voice lacked conviction. "You're a mentally unstable woman with a history of traumatic brain injury. Your perceptions can't be trusted."

"Maybe not mine alone," Emma agreed. "But what about Natalie's testimony? What about the physical evidence in your lab? What about the bodies, Alex? The ones that didn't survive your 'treatments'?"

Alex's composure cracked further, sweat beading on his forehead despite the chill in the air. "You're making things up. Confusing reality with—"

"With what?" Marcus demanded. "The false reality you created? The one you've been living in for years?"

Emma took another step forward, close enough now that the syringe in Alex's hand was just inches from her neck. She could see the yellowish liquid inside, the instrument of her captivity for all these years. The sight of it sent a shiver of revulsion through her, but she held her ground.

"It's over, Alex," she said softly, allowing herself to feel pity for the broken man before her. "The truth is out. You can't control the narrative anymore."

Something in Alex seemed to snap at her words. His face contorted with rage, and he lunged forward with the syringe, aiming for the exposed skin of her neck.

"I decide when it's over!" he shouted, his voice cracking with desperation.

Everything happened at once. Marcus moved to intercept Alex, grabbing his wrist just as the cottage door burst open with a crash that rivaled the thunder outside. Cold rain and wind swept in, carrying with them a flood of figures in dark jackets.

"Federal agents! Drop your weapons!" a commanding voice shouted above the storm's roar.

Blue and red lights splashed across the whitewashed walls, painting the small room in alternating hues. Alex froze, the syringe still clutched in his hand, his face a mask of disbelief.

"This isn't possible," he whispered. "You're bluffing. This isn't real."

"It's real, Alex," came a familiar voice from the doorway. Naomi Chen stepped into view, her dark hair plastered to her head from the rain, her face set with determination. "Everything Emma told you was true. We've been building a case against you for months."

Agents swarmed into the small space, securing Alex with swift efficiency. The syringe and gun were removed from his unresisting hands, placed carefully into evidence bags. Through it all, Alex stared at Emma with a mixture of betrayal and dawning horror.

"You couldn't have done this," he said, his voice small and confused. "You couldn't have remembered enough to—"

"To what?" Emma asked. "To fight back? To reclaim my mind? You never understood the human brain as well as you thought, Alex. Some connections are too strong to erase."

As the agents led Alex away, reading him his rights over the howl of the storm, Emma felt Marcus's arms encircle her from behind. She leaned back against his chest, feeling the steady rhythm of his heart-beat, the solid warmth of him anchoring her to reality—her reality, not the false one Alex had constructed.

"It's over," Marcus murmured against her hair. "It's really over."

Emma turned in his arms, looking up into the face she had loved and lost and found again. Rain dripped from his hair, running in rivulets down his scarred cheek. She reached up to trace the jagged line with her fingertips, each ridge and valley a piece of his story, unaltered and true.

"Not over," she corrected gently. "Just beginning. Again."

His smile broke like sunrise after the longest night, warming her from the inside out. When he lowered his lips to hers, Emma felt the final pieces of her fractured mind clicking into place. This kiss held no artifice, no manipulation—just the raw, honest connection of two people who had found their way back to each other against impossible odds.

Outside, the storm began to abate, the furious winds giving way to a steady, cleansing rain. The lighthouse beam continued its endless circuit, sweeping over the cottage every few seconds, a rhythm as familiar to Emma as her own heartbeat.

As Marcus held her, Emma realized that true perfection existed not in Alex's sterile constructs, but in this moment—rain-soaked, exhausted, but finally, unequivocally free.

CHAPTER 15 - UNRAVELING THE WEB

Emma pressed her forehead against the cool glass of the passenger window, watching the federal investigation unfold across Tidemark's manicured lawn. The mansion that had been her prison for five years now crawled with agents in windbreakers emblazoned with bold white letters: FBI, DEA, FDA. In the harsh morning light, the Sterling estate looked different—smaller somehow, its grandeur diminished by the truth now being excavated from its depths.

"Are you okay?" Marcus asked, his voice gentle in the quiet cab of his truck.

Emma turned to him, studying the familiar lines of his face. The scar along his jaw caught the sunlight, a silver reminder of the night Alex had tried to silence him forever. She reached out, her fingers hovering just above the mark before lightly tracing its path.

"I don't know what 'okay' feels like anymore," she admitted. "How do I know which parts of me are real and which parts Alex created?"

Marcus caught her hand, bringing her fingertips to his lips. His touch sent a whisper of warmth through her skin, a sensation that felt genuine in a way she was learning to recognize. "You'll figure it out. One memory at a time."

"And if I never do?" The question escaped her lips before she could stop it. "What if some parts of me stay lost forever?"

His eyes—storm-gray and honest—held hers. "Then we'll build something new. Something true."

The promise settled around her shoulders like a blanket, offering comfort she wasn't yet sure she deserved. Five years of living someone else's design had left her uncertain of her right to any future at all.

A knock on the window startled them both. Agent Naomi Chen stood outside, her dark hair pulled back in a severe ponytail, her expression professionally neutral despite the extraordinary circumstances.

Marcus rolled down his window. "What's happening in there?"

"You should see this," Naomi replied, her voice tight with controlled anger. "Both of you."

Emma hesitated only a moment before stepping out into the crisp morning air. The breeze carried the scent of salt and pine, so different from the sterile, artificially floral atmosphere Alex had maintained inside Tidemark. She took Marcus's hand as they followed Naomi up the stone pathway to the front entrance.

The foyer's marble floor echoed with footsteps as agents moved between rooms with purpose. Emma's gaze drifted up the sweeping staircase she had ascended and descended countless times, always under Alex's watchful eye. How many of those trips had been taken with a mind clouded by his chemicals?

"I used to count the steps," she murmured to Marcus. "Twenty-three. I'd count them every time, like I was afraid they might change when I wasn't looking."

"You were fighting it," he said softly. "Some part of you knew something wasn't right."

"This way," Naomi directed, leading them past the formal living room toward a door Emma had always been told led to storage.

"I was never allowed down here," Emma whispered to Marcus.

"For good reason," Naomi responded grimly, punching a code into a keypad hidden behind a painting—a seascape Emma had always found oddly compelling. The wall slid away, revealing a staircase descending into clinical brightness.

The basement laboratory sprawled beneath the entire mansion, a stark contrast to the traditional elegance above. Stainless steel gleamed under harsh fluorescent lighting. Glass-doored refrigeration units hummed along one wall, their contents visible: rows of labeled vials containing amber liquid—the same color as what had been in Alex's syringe the night before.

Emma's breath caught as memories flashed behind her eyes—Alex approaching with a smile, a glass of wine, a kiss goodnight—each moment now suspect, each tenderness potentially laced with chemical deception. "He was manufacturing the compounds here," Naomi explained as they moved deeper into the space. "Preliminary tests match the chemical signatures found in your blood samples from the hospital, Emma."

Emma's fingers tightened around Marcus's as they approached a central workstation. The touch of his skin against hers was the only real thing in this nightmare—warm, solid, present. Computer monitors displayed chemical formulas and brain scans—some labeled with her name, others with initials she didn't recognize.

"How many?" Marcus asked, his voice hoarse.

"We've identified twenty-three potential victims so far," Naomi replied, gesturing toward a locked cabinet now standing open. Inside, neat rows of files bore names and dates spanning nearly a decade. "Some were patients at his clinic. Others were people he encountered through various means—conferences, social events."

"People like me," Emma murmured.

"People he found... interesting," Naomi corrected, her professional demeanor slipping just enough to reveal her disgust. "People whose lives he could insert himself into and reshape according to his vision."

Emma released Marcus's hand and moved to a wall of photographs she hadn't noticed initially. The absence of his touch left her cold. Clinical before-and-after images showed men and women in various states of apparent confusion or clarity. Handwritten notes detailed "progress" and "setbacks." Her own face appeared in multiple frames, the earliest showing her clearly disoriented, eyes vacant, a stark contrast to later images where she smiled at the camera with manufactured happiness.

She touched one of the photos—a woman she might have been, once. Hair loose, eyes wild with confusion, a calendar visible in the background dating three weeks after her supposed car accident.

"I don't remember this," she whispered. "I thought I was still in the hospital then."

"You were here," Naomi said quietly. "In what he called the 'transition phase.'"

Emma's stomach twisted into a tight knot. "Transition from who I was to who he wanted me to be."

"This is where he perfected his techniques," Naomi continued. "Using a combination of neurochemical compounds and sophisticated psychological conditioning to alter memory formation and recall."

"He called it 'editing reality,'" Emma said quietly, the phrase rising unbidden from some corner of her mind. "He told me once, when I was half-asleep. I thought it was just a strange dream."

"It wasn't a dream," Naomi confirmed, leading them to another section of the laboratory. "This is where he maintained the control center for your daily life."

Screens displayed feeds from hidden cameras throughout Tide-mark—the bedroom, kitchen, even the bathroom. A separate monitor showed Emma's vital signs, tracked through the fitness watch Alex had insisted she wear "for her health." Beside these, a meticulous schedule outlined daily medication doses adjusted based on her activities, moods, and sleep patterns.

"He was monitoring everything," Marcus said, his voice tight with barely controlled rage. His hand found the small of Emma's back, protective and steadying.

"Everything," Naomi agreed. "And when your genuine memories started breaking through, Emma, he adjusted the chemical balance to strengthen the false ones."

Emma approached a desk where journals lay open, filled with Alex's precise handwriting. She recognized his perfectionist script immediately—the same hand that had signed countless love notes she'd found throughout the house, notes she'd convinced herself were romantic rather than calculating.

"He documented everything," she whispered, scanning the pages. "Like I was just another experiment."

"You were his masterpiece," Marcus said, reading over her shoulder. "That's what he writes here. His greatest achievement."

Emma's fingers trembled as she turned a page. "'Subject continues to accept implanted narratives regarding our relationship. Emotional anchoring techniques particularly effective when paired with compound NSC-42. Note: Increase dosage when subject exhibits independent thinking.'"

The clinical assessment of her mind, her very self, written in such cold, detached language, sent a wave of nausea through Emma. She stepped back from the desk, bumping into a filing cabinet. Marcus caught her elbow, steadying her with gentle hands.

"There's something else you should see," Naomi said gently, guiding Emma to a small room off the main laboratory.

The space resembled a comfortable study—bookshelves lined the walls, two leather chairs faced each other across a coffee table, soft lighting created a warm atmosphere. A stark contrast to the clinical environment just outside its door.

"This is where he conducted his 'therapy sessions' with you," Naomi explained. "Where he would reinforce the false memories while you were in a chemically susceptible state."

Emma's eyes were drawn to a familiar book on the coffee table—a photo album bound in blue leather. With trembling fingers, she opened it, revealing wedding pictures. Her in a flowing white dress, Alex handsome in a tuxedo, both smiling against a backdrop of Tidemark's cliffside garden.

"I remember this day," Emma said, her voice breaking. "I remember the taste of champagne, the weight of the dress, the way he whispered 'forever' when we danced." She looked up, eyes brimming with tears that caught the soft light. "None of it happened, did it?"

Marcus knelt beside her chair, taking her hands in his. His thumbs traced gentle circles on her skin, an intimacy that felt real in a room built for lies. "No," he said softly. "But what's happening now is real. You finding the truth. You finding yourself again." "They're expertly manipulated images," Naomi confirmed. "His team found evidence of extensive digital alteration."

Emma closed the album, unable to bear the sight of that radiant, deluded woman who both was and wasn't her. Every cherished memory now suspect, every moment of happiness potentially falsified.

"What about Lily?" Emma asked suddenly, panic rising in her throat. "Is she—?"

"She's your daughter," Marcus assured her quickly, taking her hands in his. "Our daughter. The DNA tests already confirmed it. But Alex altered her memories too, made her believe he was her father."

"She's safe," Naomi added. "Child services has her with a specialized trauma counselor. They're being very gentle with her, helping her understand what's real."

Emma nodded, relief washing through her even as fresh anger ignited. Alex had manipulated not just her mind but her child's as well. The cruelty of it staggered her.

"I want to see her," Emma said firmly.

"Soon," Naomi promised. "The counselor wants to prepare her first. It's a lot for a four-year-old to process."

They returned to the main laboratory, where agents were carefully cataloging evidence, photographing equipment, downloading files from computers. The scope of Alex's operation was becoming clearer with each passing minute.

"What about the other victims?" Marcus asked, his arm protective around Emma's shoulders.

"We're contacting them now," Naomi replied. "Some have been under his influence for years. Others were more... short-term experiments. Not everyone responded to the treatments as successfully as Emma." Her voice lowered. "Some suffered permanent neurological damage."

"And some died," Emma said quietly, remembering Alex's words from the night before.

Naomi nodded grimly. "We're excavating a section of the property near the north woods. Ground-penetrating radar showed... anomalies."

The weight of it all threatened to crush Emma. How many lives had Alex destroyed in his quest to perfect his techniques? How many people had suffered so he could create his ideal reality?

"I need air," she said suddenly, turning toward the stairs.

Marcus followed her up and out of the mansion, past curious agents and into the garden where the morning sun had finally warmed the rain-soaked grounds. Emma took deep breaths, filling her lungs with fresh, untainted air.

"Everything I thought I knew about myself for the past five years was fabricated," she said, her voice surprisingly steady. "My marriage, my home, even my basic preferences—all designed by him."

Marcus kept a respectful distance, giving her the space to process. "Not everything," he said softly. "He couldn't erase all of you, Emma. That's why you kept fighting back. Why you found your way to the lighthouse, to Naomi, to me. Your true self kept surfacing, despite everything he did."

Emma turned to face him, studying his features in the clear morning light. Unlike the manufactured memories of Alex, which now seemed to shimmer and dissolve when she focused on them, her memories of Marcus felt solid, anchored in reality.

"I remember the first time I met you," she said slowly, testing the memory's authenticity. "At the harbor, three years before the accident. You were fixing the lighthouse keeper's boat. You had wood shavings in your hair."

Marcus smiled, the expression transforming his serious face. "You brushed them away and told me I looked like I'd been caught in a sawdust storm."

The memory felt different from the implanted ones—richer, filled with sensory details Alex couldn't have known to include. The smell of sawdust and motor oil, the way the late afternoon sun had caught in Marcus's hair, the surprising roughness of his hands when they'd shaken in greeting.

"I fell in love with you over sea glass," Emma continued, the memory unfurling itself with startling clarity. "We collected it on the beach, and you made me that pendant—"

"The blue-green piece shaped like a teardrop," Marcus finished, reaching into his pocket. "I kept it after... after Alex took you away. I carried it everywhere." He held out his hand, revealing a smooth, weathered piece of sea glass on his palm, wrapped in simple silver wire.

Emma took it with trembling fingers, the cool weight of it familiar against her skin. This was real. This connection was real. She closed her eyes, letting genuine memories wash over her—stargazing from the lighthouse keeper's cottage, Marcus teaching her to carve wood, planning their future together when her investigation of Sterling Neuroscience was complete.

When she opened her eyes, Marcus was watching her with such tenderness it made her heart ache.

"We'll find our way back," he promised quietly. "Not to what we were—we can't erase these five years. But to something new, something true."

His words settled over her like a soft rain, washing away some of the poison Alex had poured into her life. Not a cure—nothing would ever fully undo what had been done—but the beginning of healing.

The sound of approaching footsteps interrupted them. Naomi appeared, holding a stack of files.

"Emma, there's something else we found," she said, her professional tone unable to completely mask her concern. "Medical files. About your pregnancy with Lily."

Emma felt her blood run cold. "What about it?"

"Alex documented everything," Naomi explained gently. "It appears he discovered you were pregnant shortly after... after he took you. The child was clearly Marcus's, but he saw it as an opportunity."

"An opportunity?" Marcus echoed, his voice dangerous.

"To cement his false reality," Naomi continued. "He adjusted your treatments throughout the pregnancy, gradually convincing you the child was his. After Lily was born, he extended the treatments to include her, using age-appropriate techniques to shape her understanding of family."

Emma felt sick. "He manipulated an infant's developing mind? Is she—will she be—?"

"The specialists believe children her age are remarkably resilient," Naomi assured her. "And the treatments she received were much milder than yours. With proper support, she should fully recover her authentic attachment to you both."

Emma turned away, gazing across Tidemark's expansive grounds to where the lighthouse stood in the distance, its white tower gleaming in the morning sun. For five years, that beacon had called to her, tugging at the buried truth in her mind. Now it represented something else—a fixed point of reality in a world that had proven dangerously malleable.

"I want to go home," she said suddenly.

Marcus and Naomi exchanged glances.

"Tidemark?" Naomi asked cautiously.

"No," Emma said firmly. "The lighthouse cottage. That's where I belong. Where we belong," she added, looking at Marcus.

His smile then—tentative but warm, like sunrise breaking through clouds—told her everything she needed to know about the road ahead. It would be difficult, this rebuilding of life and trust, but they would walk it together, one true memory at a time.

CHAPTER 16 – LILY'S LULLABY

"It's okay to be quiet for as long as you need," Dr. Marisol Patel said, her voice as warm as the chamomile tea steaming in Emma's hands. "There's no hurry."

Emma sat beside Marcus on a small sofa designed for parents, close enough that their shoulders touched but not so close that Lily might feel pressured by their attention. The cushion between them held their unspoken fears—a small valley of uncertainty. Three sessions had passed with minimal progress—Lily drawing pictures, playing with sand trays, but speaking only in whispers to Dr. Patel when Emma and Marcus stepped out.

Emma studied the room, taking in details to calm her racing heart: the soft blue walls adorned with children's artwork, shelves lined with toys and books, and the gentle bubbling of a small aquarium in the corner. Light filtered through gauzy curtains, casting a hazy glow over everything. The office was designed for comfort, for safety—everything their lives had lacked these past months.

Today marked their first full family session. Dr. Patel had called that morning, her voice carefully measured: "Lily's ready to share some important things with you both." Even through the phone, Emma had detected the subtle note of cautious optimism.

Now, watching her daughter's serious face—so like Marcus's when deep in thought—Emma fought the instinct to gather the child into her arms. Lily sat cross-legged on a round carpet patterned with woodland creatures, her small fingers clutching a purple octopus plush that had once been inseparable from her. Dr. Patel had been clear: let Lily lead this dance.

"Can I tell them about the pretend game?" Lily asked Dr. Patel, her voice small but steady.

"If you're ready," Dr. Patel nodded, settling cross-legged on a cushion between Lily and her parents.

Emma felt Marcus tense beside her. His breathing had gone shallow, his right hand clenching and unclenching in a rhythm she recognized from their life before—when storms approached the lighthouse and he worried about the boats at sea. Some habits survived even the worst upheavals.

Lily took a deep breath that seemed to expand her entire tiny frame. Her eyes—liquid brown with flecks of amber, just like her father's—darted between her parents before fixing firmly on her plush toy.

"Daddy—I mean, Dr. Alex—told me we had to play a special game with Mommy." Her eyes flicked up to Emma's face, then back to the octopus. "He said Mommy got hurt in her head and forgot things, and we had to help her remember the right way."

Emma's fingers tightened around her mug, the ceramic suddenly too hot against her skin. The room seemed to contract, the walls pressing closer. Marcus's hand found hers, his thumb tracing gentle circles against her skin—an anchor in the rising tide of her horror.

"What was the right way, sweetheart?" Dr. Patel prompted when Lily fell silent, her calm voice a counterpoint to the tension threading the air.

"That he was my daddy. That they loved each other very, very much. That we were a happy family." Lily's voice gained strength with each statement, as if relieved to finally speak these words aloud. Her fingers worked methodically through the octopus's tentacles, straightening and smoothing each fabric limb. "He made me practice every morning before Mommy woke up. We'd sit in the kitchen, and he'd ask questions like, 'Who is your daddy?' and 'How long have we been a family?'"

Emma swallowed hard against the knot in her throat. How many mornings had she awakened to find Lily already dressed, already perfect, sitting quietly at the breakfast table with that solemn expression? The breakfast table in that beautiful house—a house she now realized she'd never actually chosen.

"He had answers I had to remember," Lily continued, her voice dropping to a whisper. "If I forgot or said the wrong thing, he'd get the scary eyes."

"The scary eyes?" Dr. Patel asked gently.

Lily nodded vigorously. "When they go all dark and tight, like this." She demonstrated, narrowing her eyes and pressing her lips together in such a perfect mimicry of Alex that Emma felt cold wash over her skin.

"And if you didn't play the game right?" Marcus asked softly, his voice rough with controlled emotion.

"Time-outs in the blue room," Lily whispered. "With the special medicine that made me sleepy."

Emma felt her heart crack, jagged pieces scraping against her ribs. The blue room—Alex's home office, always locked, always forbidden. How many punishments had her daughter endured while Emma moved through the house in a chemically-induced haze, oblivious to the manipulation happening around her?

"Sometimes," Lily added, her voice smaller still, "if I was really bad, he'd say Mommy needed extra medicine in her tea. Then she'd sleep all afternoon, and he'd say it was my fault for upsetting her."

The teacup trembled in Emma's hands. Marcus gently took it from her and set it aside, his fingers lingering on hers. In that touch was a promise—one they'd made long ago, standing before a justice of the peace with the lighthouse as their witness: I'll hold you through the storm.

"You're being so brave telling us this," Emma managed, her voice thick with emotion.

Lily looked up, her eyes—Marcus's eyes—suddenly fierce. "I knew it wasn't real. I knew you weren't his. Even when I had to say the words, in my head I always knew."

"How did you know that, Lily?" Dr. Patel asked, leaning forward slightly, her silver-framed glasses catching the light.

"Because of the pictures in my head." Lily tapped her temple with a small finger. "The old pictures, from before. Dr. Alex couldn't take all of them away with his special medicine."

Emma caught her breath. The "special medicine"—the drops Alex had insisted Lily needed for her anxiety, administered nightly with her water. How had she not questioned it more forcefully? But she knew the answer: her own "medication" had clouded her judgment, dulled her maternal instincts, made her compliant. Like a puppet with her strings pulled taut, she had moved through those months in a haze, never quite connecting the fragments of doubt that occasionally pierced the fog.

"What pictures do you remember, sweetheart?" Marcus leaned forward, his voice gentle but threaded with urgency. His fingers had gone white-knuckled around Emma's hand, but his face remained composed for Lily's sake—that careful mask he'd always worn when trying to shield their daughter from worry.

Lily's face brightened, a glimpse of sunshine breaking through storm clouds. "The lighthouse. And you." She pointed at Marcus with absolute certainty. "You used to throw me up in the air and catch me. And we lived in the little house by the water, and Mommy would sing the octopus song when it was stormy."

Emma gasped softly, a sharp intake of breath that sounded too loud in the quiet room. The octopus song—a nonsense tune she'd invented during Lily's infancy, when thunderstorms made her fussy. Alex couldn't have known about it; it belonged to their real life, before the nightmare began. Before he stole them away, one memory at a time.

"Sometimes I'd hum it real quiet," Lily continued, "when Dr. Alex wasn't listening. It helped me remember the lighthouse and the waves and how Daddy—real Daddy—smells like wood and salt."

Marcus made a choked sound beside Emma, quickly masked with a cough. His free hand rose to his face, thumb pressing hard against the corner of his eye. Emma could feel the tremor in his fingers where they clutched hers, a physical manifestation of the storm raging inside him.

"That's why I kept drawing the lighthouse," Lily explained earnestly. "I thought maybe if Mommy saw enough pictures, she'd remember too."

Emma's mind flashed to the countless drawings Lily had created over the past year—the tall structure appearing again and again. Alex had frowned at them, suggesting gentler subjects for a little girl. Once, he'd even crumpled one up, citing "unhealthy fixation." The memory sent a chill of rage through Emma's veins.

"What else do you remember about Marcus?" Dr. Patel asked, her voice measured and professional, though Emma caught a flicker of emotion behind her composed expression.

"That he's my real daddy." Lily stated it simply, a fact as obvious as the color of the sky. "I always knew, even when Dr. Alex said I was wrong. The lighthouse man is my daddy."

The simple phrase—"lighthouse man"—struck Emma with the force of a wave. That's what Lily had called Marcus from the time she could speak, watching him from their cottage window as he climbed the spiral stairs for his evening shift, illuminating the darkness for ships at sea. In those days, Marcus would kiss them both goodbye, his lips lingering on Emma's, promising to return with the dawn.

"And what did you think about Dr. Alex?" Dr. Patel continued carefully, watching Lily's face.

Lily's expression darkened, her small fingers gripping the octopus tighter against her chest. "He was the monster in the white coat," she whispered. "Like in the stories. The one who wanted to keep the princess locked in the tower forever."

A shiver traced Emma's spine, raising goosebumps along her arms. The fairy tales she'd read to Lily—had her daughter been interpreting them as their reality all along? Had she understood more than any of them realized?

"Dr. Alex said if I told Mommy about the game, she would get sick again and have to go to the hospital forever." Lily's voice trembled, and for the first time since they'd entered the room, tears gathered in her

eyes. "He said they'd take me away to a special school for children who
tell lies."

Emma bit the inside of her cheek hard enough to taste copper.
Beside her, Marcus's breathing had gone dangerously steady—the
controlled rhythm he used when navigating his boat through the worst
storms. She knew that steadiness, remembered it from nights when
gales lashed their little cottage and he'd hold her close, whispering that
the lighthouse would guide them through.

"But I left clues," Lily added, a note of fierce pride entering her
voice. "I drew pictures. I whispered things when he wasn't listening.
I put my secret drawings under your pillow, Mommy."

"The drawings under my pillow," Emma whispered, memory crystallizing. The stick figures she'd found—a woman and child in a lighthouse with a scarred man, while a doctor figure stood outside. She'd
been so confused, had almost shown them to Alex. Some instinct had
stopped her, some buried part of her true self fighting to be heard.

Lily nodded vigorously, her curls bouncing. "I was trying to help
you remember. Like how you used to help me remember my letters."

"You were very clever," Marcus said, his voice thick with pride and
pain. His thumb stroked the back of Emma's hand, a familiar touch
that now felt like coming home after years adrift.

"I knew you were fighting the spell," Lily continued earnestly. "Like
in Sleeping Beauty. I heard you talking in your sleep sometimes, calling
for Daddy—my real daddy. And then you started going to the lighthouse, and I knew the spell was breaking."

Emma recalled those midnight walks she'd taken, drawn to the
lighthouse by some force she couldn't explain—her true self fighting through the chemical fog. And Lily had been watching, hoping,
believing in her even when she'd lost belief in herself. The thought
made tears sting her eyes, hot and sudden. In the darkness of Alex's

deception, her daughter had been a tiny flame of truth, refusing to be extinguished.

"Were you scared, living with Dr. Alex?" Dr. Patel asked carefully, her pen poised above her notepad.

Lily considered this, her head tilted thoughtfully, one finger tapping against the octopus's head. "Only when he got the angry eyes. When Mommy didn't take her special tea or when she talked about the lighthouse too much."

"You noticed all of that?" Emma couldn't help asking, astounded by her daughter's perception.

"I'm very good at watching," Lily said with a child's simple pride. "That's what Dr. Alex didn't know. I pretended to be little and silly, but I was watching everything." She straightened her shoulders slightly. "Like when he put the medicine in your food when you weren't looking. Or when he took away the picture frames from the hall cabinet when you were sleeping."

Marcus shifted forward, his movement careful and slow as if approaching a fawn in the woods. "Lily, can I ask you something important?"

She nodded solemnly, her eyes suddenly wary.

"Are you afraid of me now? It's been a long time since we were together at the lighthouse."

The question hung in the air, delicate as morning mist. Emma held her breath, acutely aware of what this moment meant to Marcus—this man who had lost everything, who had been erased from his own child's life, who had been told his wife and daughter were dead only to discover a truth far more twisted.

Lily regarded him thoughtfully, studying his face—the scar along his jaw from the boating accident that had kept him from home that fateful night, the worry lines at his eyes, the weathered skin tanned by years of sea and sun. Then, with the decisive certainty that only children possess, she slid from her chair and crossed the small space to stand before him.

"You're still my daddy," she said, reaching up to touch his scar with gentle fingers. "You got this fighting the monster to save us."

Marcus's composure crumbled. Tears filled his eyes as he opened his arms in silent question. Lily climbed into his lap without hesitation, fitting herself against his chest as if returning to a familiar home after a long absence.

"I kept your shell collection safe," he whispered into her hair, his voice raw. "All the ones we found together."

"The purple one too?" Lily asked, her voice muffled against his shirt.

"Especially the purple one. It's still on your windowsill, catching the morning light."

Emma watched them, this reunion of father and daughter, feeling both witness to and part of something precious. Lily's resilience stunned her—this tiny being who had carried truth through a storm of manipulation, who had kept her genuine self alive despite everything.

"There's something else Lily wanted to tell you both," Dr. Patel said gently after giving them a moment. "Something important about moving forward."

Lily pulled back from Marcus's embrace, her expression suddenly serious again. "I want to go home to the lighthouse," she announced. "Not to the big scary house. I want my real room back with the stars on the ceiling."

Emma and Marcus exchanged glances. They had discussed this endlessly over the past weeks—where to live, how to rebuild, what would be best for Lily's recovery. The lighthouse keeper's cottage was small, in need of repairs after years of neglect. The practical choice would be finding a new home, one without connections to either past.

"The lighthouse cottage is very small," Emma said carefully. "And it needs a lot of work before anyone could live there again."

"But it's our home," Lily insisted, her lower lip trembling slightly. "And the ocean can wash away the bad dreams. That's what you always said, Mommy."

Another genuine memory, another thread connecting them to their authentic past. Emma felt tears prick her eyes.

"We could fix it up," Marcus said quietly to Emma. "I've already started on the roof and windows."

"You have?" Emma turned to him, surprised.

He nodded, a faint flush coloring his cheeks. "I've gone there most evenings after leaving you at the hotel. It gave me something to do with my hands while waiting for—" he glanced at Lily, "—for everything to sort itself out."

"He fixed my window seat," Lily said with certainty, though she couldn't possibly know. "The one where I could watch the boats."

Marcus's eyes widened slightly. "How did you know that?"

"I just did," Lily shrugged, as if the knowledge were as natural as breathing. "Is there really still a star ceiling?"

Marcus smiled, the expression transforming his weather-worn face. "The glow-in-the-dark stars are still there. A little faded, but nothing a few new ones couldn't fix."

"And my shell collection?"

"In a box under the window seat, right where you left it."

Lily turned to Emma, her eyes wide and hopeful. "Can we go there today? Just to see?"

Emma looked to Dr. Patel, who nodded slightly. "A short visit might be beneficial. Reconnecting with positive spaces from before the trauma can help rebuild authentic attachment."

"Then yes," Emma decided, the word feeling right as it left her lips. "We can go see the lighthouse today."

Lily's smile—Marcus's smile—bloomed across her face. "And maybe stay for a sleepover?"

"We'll see," Emma hedged, though something in her yearned for it too—to fall asleep to the rhythm of waves against the shore, to wake in a place that had known her true self.

"Before we end our session," Dr. Patel said, "Lily has made something she wants to share with you both."

From a shelf behind her, Dr. Patel retrieved a colorful construction paper creation—a book bound with yarn through punched holes. The cover, decorated with glitter and seashell stickers, read "My Real Family" in Lily's careful printing.

"I made a truth book," Lily explained seriously as she handed it to Emma. "So we don't forget again."

Emma opened it carefully, mindful of the fragile binding. Each page held crayon drawings—three figures standing by a lighthouse, fishing from rocks, building sandcastles. Beneath each picture, in Dr. Patel's neat adult handwriting, were Lily's words: "This is my mom and dad at our real home." "We catch fish together for dinner." "We look for treasure on the beach."

The images were vivid with detail only a child who had lived these moments could include—the exact pattern of stones on the lighthouse path, the way Marcus's hair stuck up in the back when wet with sea spray, the red rubber boots Emma wore for tide-pooling.

On the final page, Lily had drawn what appeared to be the three of them holding hands in a circle, a giant red heart surrounding them. Beneath it was written: "The monster tried to make us forget, but love is stronger than special medicine."

"This is beautiful, Lily," Emma managed to say, her throat tight with emotion.

CHAPTER 17 - FRACTURED FOUNDATIONS

T he lighthouse beam no longer haunted Emma's dreams. After a year of healing, its steady rhythm had transformed from an accusation into a comfort—a metronome marking time regained rather than time lost. She curled her fingers around the ceramic mug, its warmth seeping into hands that had grown stronger since she'd begun renovating the cottage herself.

"You're up early," Marcus's voice came from behind her, sleep-roughened and tender.

Emma turned, taking in the sight of him in the doorway—hair tousled, wearing flannel pajama pants and the faded University of Maine T-shirt she'd bought him last month. The scar along his jaw caught the morning light, no longer a reminder of the night Alex had tried to eliminate him, but rather proof of his survival. Their survival.

"Couldn't sleep," she admitted. "The publisher called yesterday. 'Memory's Veil' just hit number one."

A slow smile spread across Marcus's face as he crossed to her. "Dr. Walker becomes a bestselling author. I'm hardly surprised." His arms encircled her waist, his chin resting atop her head as they both gazed out at the ocean. "You've always had important things to say."

The cottage kitchen filled with the scent of brewing coffee and sea air drifting through the half-open window. Emma leaned back against his chest, feeling the steady thump of his heart. Every beat seemed to whisper her name, a quiet affirmation that they'd found their way back to each other.

"Three more universities have established ethics panels based on the book's recommendations," she said, tracing her finger along the rim of her mug. "The Senate committee hearing is next month."

"Proud of you," he murmured against her hair, his breath warm against her scalp.

Emma closed her eyes, savoring the sensation. These small moments of closeness still felt like miracles after what they'd endured. Every morning she woke half-expecting the cottage walls to dissolve around her, revealing Alex's mansion and his carefully constructed lies. But the weathered floorboards remained solid beneath her feet, the salt-tinged air real in her lungs.

"The wood for the porch railings arrives today," she said, changing the subject. "I thought we might paint them that seafoam color Lily picked out."

Marcus chuckled, the sound reverberating through his chest and into hers. "Our daughter, the decorator. Though I have to admit, she has better taste than I do."

"Than both of us," Emma corrected with a smile. "Remember the orange curtains in our first apartment?"

"God, those were awful. Like someone had skinned a traffic cone."

They laughed together, the sound filling the kitchen's rafters. Emma treasured these reclaimed memories, the ones that had stayed buried in her mind despite Alex's manipulations. Each one that resurfaced felt like finding a rare shell intact on the shoreline.

"Is Lily still asleep?" Emma asked, glancing toward the hallway that led to their daughter's room.

"Out like a light. That science project wore her out."

Emma smiled, remembering their daughter's intense concentration as she cataloged the tide pool specimens they'd collected yesterday. At eight years old, Lily showed every sign of following her mother into marine biology, her natural curiosity having survived intact.

"She reminds me so much of you," Marcus said softly, as if reading her thoughts. "The way her forehead crinkles when she's thinking. The little notes she leaves everywhere."

"Poor thing, inheriting my terrible handwriting."

"It's not terrible. It's distinctive." He pressed a kiss to the top of her head. "Like everything about you."

"The real estate agent called again," Marcus said, his tone carefully neutral. "Someone else is interested in Tidemark."

Emma's shoulders tensed momentarily before she forced them to relax. Alex's mansion—now legally hers after the settlement—remained empty on the cliffs, a monument to deception she couldn't bring herself to visit.

"Tell her to proceed with the offer," Emma decided, turning to face him. "The foundation could use the funds."

His eyes—those warm brown depths flecked with amber, just like Lily's—searched hers. "You're sure? You don't need more time to think about it?"

Emma shook her head, setting her mug on the counter. "I've had enough time. That house was never real to me—just a stage set for Alex's fantasy. The money will help people who need it."

The Emma Walker Foundation for Memory Trauma Recovery had become her mission alongside her writing—supporting victims of psychological manipulation with specialized therapy and legal assistance. Twenty-three survivors of Alex's experiments now received treatment through its programs, with more coming forward as the criminal case against him proceeded.

"Besides," she continued, "there's something fitting about using his money to undo his damage."

Marcus tucked a strand of hair behind her ear, his fingers lingering against her cheek. "Always the writer beneath the scientist."

"Only with you," she whispered.

His expression softened as he lowered his mouth to hers in a kiss that began as comfort but quickly transformed into something more urgent. Emma's hands slipped beneath his shirt, tracing the familiar landscape of his back, relearning what had been temporarily forgotten. The heat of his skin against her palms anchored her to the present moment.

When they parted, both slightly breathless, Marcus pressed his forehead to hers. "Coffee first, or walk on the beach?"

"Beach," Emma decided. "The tide's perfect for sea glass."

They moved through their morning routine with the easy rhythm of those who have found their way back to each other—Marcus starting coffee while Emma pulled two well-worn sweaters from hooks by the door. She slipped into her boots, wiggling her toes against the sheepskin lining.

"I'll leave a note for Lily," Marcus said, scribbling on the chalkboard they kept by the refrigerator.

Outside, the air carried the sharp scent of salt and seaweed. Emma breathed deeply, filling her lungs with the fragrance of genuine memories. They walked hand in hand down the weathered steps to the small, private cove below the lighthouse, their feet finding familiar paths among the rocks.

"I've been thinking about your offer," Emma said as they reached the shoreline, where gentle waves lapped against smooth stones.

Marcus raised an eyebrow, bending to retrieve a piece of blue sea glass. "Which one?"

"The research vessel. Taking it out next summer for the Gulf of Maine project."

His face brightened, a smile spreading slow and genuine across his features. Before Alex, they had often worked together—Marcus navigating difficult waters while Emma conducted her research. The prospect of returning to their shared professional life represented another piece of normalcy reclaimed.

"The Emilia would love to have you back," he said, referencing the boat he'd named for her years ago. "She's not the same without you cataloging specimens in the cabin and leaving coffee mugs everywhere."

Emma laughed, the sound carrying across the water. "I'm very organized now. Recovery side effect, according to Dr. Patel."

"The woman who can't find her phone three times a day is claiming to be organized?" His teasing was gentle, wrapped in affection.

"That's different," Emma protested. "Phones are sneaky. They move when you're not looking."

Marcus's expression softened as he pulled her close again. "You can reorganize my entire boat if it makes you happy."

They stood in comfortable silence, watching the waves retreat and advance. Emma collected several pieces of sea glass—emerald, cobalt, and amber—tucking them into her pocket for Lily's collection. The morning sun strengthened, burning away the last wisps of fog.

"I thought about him yesterday," Emma admitted, her voice quiet against the backdrop of surf. "Alex."

Marcus waited, giving her space to continue, his hand warm and steady around hers.

"Not with fear this time. With pity." She stared out at the horizon, where the sky met the ocean in a clean line. "To be so brilliant and so empty inside that he had to steal lives rather than build his own."

"The prosecution says he'll never leave psychiatric detention," Marcus said. "Too dangerous."

Emma nodded. Alex's trial had unveiled the full scope of his obsession—journals chronicling years of stalking her, elaborate plans for eliminating Marcus, and disturbing experiments on patients who resembled her. The memory manipulation techniques he'd pioneered had won him professional acclaim while masking his increasingly dangerous fixations.

"I don't want Lily to testify," she said suddenly, turning to face him. "I know the prosecutor thinks her statement would secure additional charges, but—"

"I already told them no," Marcus interrupted gently. "She's healing. That's all that matters."

Relief washed through Emma, warm and swift as summer rain. She raised herself on tiptoes, pressing her lips to the scar on his jaw—a gesture that had become their ritual, an acknowledgment of what they'd endured together.

"Mom! Dad!" Lily's voice carried down from the cottage, where she stood on the porch in mismatched pajamas, waving enthusiastically. "I found a starfish in the tank! It's changing colors!"

"We're coming, sea sprite!" Marcus called back, using the nickname that had stuck since her toddler days.

Emma smiled, watching her daughter bounce excitedly on the porch. Dr. Patel had warned them recovery wouldn't follow a straight line—there would be nightmares, setbacks, moments of confusion—but Lily had proven remarkably resilient. Like sea grass bending in storms, she had survived by adapting rather than breaking.

As they climbed back toward the cottage, Marcus paused halfway, turning to look at Emma with an expression that made her heart flutter despite their years together.

"What?" she asked, suddenly self-conscious under his gaze.

"Just remembering the first time I brought you here," he said, his voice low and intimate. "You climbed these steps in those ridiculous high-heeled boots because you thought the lighthouse keeper would be some gruff old sailor, not—"

"Not a handsome marine biologist's younger brother who looked like he belonged on the cover of 'Fisherman Monthly'?" Emma finished with a teasing smile.

Marcus laughed, the sound genuine and unreserved. "I believe you called me 'surprisingly articulate for someone who stares at waves all day.'"

"I was intimidated! You had three advanced degrees and made your own sourdough bread."

"And you had just won your second Emmy for deep-sea documentaries. Trust me, I was the intimidated one."

This was the sweetest part of recovery—rediscovering shared memories that Alex hadn't managed to erase, moments that had remained hidden beneath the surface of her consciousness like shells waiting to be uncovered at low tide. Each reclaimed memory felt like a victory, another piece of herself restored.

Inside the cottage, the day unfolded in simple, precious moments: Lily's excited explanation of her starfish's color adaptations; Marcus making blueberry pancakes shaped like sea creatures; Emma finding an old field journal filled with notes from their first summer together.

That evening, as sunset painted the sea in shades of amber and rose, Emma stood on the porch, watching Marcus and Lily build an elaborate sand castle at the water's edge. Their laughter floated up to her, carried on the salt-laden breeze.

"We need a flag, Dad!" Lily called, her hands on her hips in a posture that mirrored her mother's so precisely it made Emma's heart ache with love.

"Coming up!" Marcus retrieved a piece of driftwood, attaching Emma's discarded scarf to create a makeshift pennant.

Emma leaned against the porch railing, savoring the sight. A year ago, she had been trapped in a haze of false memories, locked in Alex's carefully constructed version of reality. Now she stood on solid ground, surrounded by authentic love.

Inside her pocket, she felt the outline of the sea glass pieces she'd collected that morning. Tomorrow, she would add them to the wind chime she was creating for the porch—a collection of colored glass that would catch the light and transform it, just as she had transformed her pain into healing.

"Mom!" Lily waved frantically. "Come see the moat! It works with real water!"

"I'll be right there!" Emma called back, already moving toward the steps.

As she crossed the sand to join her family, Emma felt the weight of the past year find its proper place—not forgotten, but no longer controlling her future. The lighthouse beam swept across the darkening sky behind them, its rhythm steady and reassuring.

Here, on this familiar shore, Emma Walker had found her way home—not to the false paradise Alex had manufactured, but to something far more valuable: a life built on truth, sustained by love, illuminated by genuine memories that no one could ever take from her again.

CHAPTER EIGHTEEN

CHAPTER 18 - LOVE IN THE LIGHT

"Look what I found!" Lily called, breaking free from her father's grasp to race toward Emma. Sand still clung to her knees, and her braids had come half-undone after their afternoon on the shore. She thrust her palm forward, revealing a perfect sand dollar, its star pattern intact. "Dad says it's lucky."

"It certainly is," Emma confirmed, accepting the delicate treasure with appropriate reverence. "Only about one in a thousand survive without breaking."

The coastal wind carried the scent of salt and seaweed as it brushed against Emma's face. She studied the fragile disk in her palm, marveling at nature's precision—five perfect oval patterns radiating from its center like some ancient symbol. Behind the sand dollar, her daughter's eyes shone with equal artistry, flecks of amber catching the late afternoon light.

Lily beamed, her face flushed with the pride of discovery. "I'm going to put it with my collection. After I wash it. Dad says it needs special cleaning or it'll fall apart."

"Your father is right about that," Emma said, glancing over her daughter's head to where Marcus approached at a more measured pace. His jeans were rolled up past his ankles, still damp at the hems, and the wind had pushed his dark hair into unruly waves. The scar along his jaw caught the last glimmer of sunset, a silver-pink line marking where his brother's rage had nearly taken him from her forever.

There was something about the way he moved—deliberate yet graceful—that still quickened Emma's pulse. Even now, after everything they'd endured, the sight of him walking toward her across the sand ignited something primal within her chest.

"I'm always right," Marcus teased, joining them on the steps. "Isn't that what you're constantly telling me, Dr. Walker?"

Emma arched an eyebrow. "I believe the phrase I use most often is 'marginally less wrong than yesterday.'"

His laugh crinkled the corners of his eyes in a way that made her want to trace the lines with her fingertips. She resisted, conscious of their daughter watching with keen interest.

Lily giggled, darting between them into the cottage, calling over her shoulder, "I'm getting my special brush for the sand dollar!"

As the screen door slapped shut behind their daughter, Marcus moved closer, his hand finding Emma's with the easy certainty that still amazed her. Even after everything—the stolen years, the false memories, the agonizing reconstruction of her identity—his touch remained familiar, a truth her body had recognized even when her mind could not.

"She had a good day," he observed quietly. "No nightmares last night either."

The warmth of his palm against hers sent tiny shivers up her arm. Emma leaned into him, allowing their shoulders to touch—a simple connection that had once seemed impossible to reclaim.

"Dr. Patel says children often recover faster than adults. Their identities are still forming, more elastic."

"Unlike their stubborn parents?" Marcus suggested with a gentle smile.

"Speak for yourself, Sterling," Emma replied, but without heat. She turned her face toward the ocean, where the lighthouse beam now cut clearly through gathering darkness. "Though I suppose I am somewhat set in my ways."

The fading light cast long shadows across the weathered boards of the porch. Above them, the first stars pierced the deepening blue of the sky, pinpricks of light against the vast emptiness.

"Hmm. Like insisting on sleeping on the left side of the bed."

"That's logical. The right side is closer to the door, and you're better at confronting potential midnight intruders."

His thumb traced small circles against her wrist, each rotation a whispered promise. "Or refusing to eat blueberries that touch other fruit."

"Cross-contamination is scientifically proven to alter flavor profiles."

The corners of his mouth twitched upward. "Very scientific, Dr. Walker."

Marcus laughed, the sound deep and unreserved. "What about your refusal to wear matching socks?"

A sudden chill that had nothing to do with the evening air crept across Emma's skin. Something in her mind shifted, like a door opening onto an empty room where furniture should be.

"That's just—" Emma paused, frowning slightly. "Wait. That's not a real memory."

The smile faded from Marcus's face as understanding dawned. "Alex?" he asked, his voice careful.

Emma nodded, unconsciously rubbing her temple where phantom pain sometimes flared when false memories surfaced. "He planted that one. Said it was our inside joke—that I was too brilliant to bother with matching socks."

A dark cloud seemed to pass between them, the name itself a shadow that could still dim the light. Marcus's fingers tightened around hers, anchoring her to the present. His touch was different from Alex's—never possessive, always steadying.

"For what it's worth, you've always been terribly particular about your socks matching. You once made us late to your own award ceremony because you couldn't find the exact right pair." The genuine memory floated up from the recesses of her mind—the frantic search through luggage in a hotel room, Marcus holding up various options while she rejected them all, both of them laughing despite the ticking clock. The scene played with such clarity that Emma could almost smell the hotel's lavender toiletries, feel the plush carpet beneath her bare feet.

"Toronto," she said suddenly. "The Environmental Media Awards. You were wearing that ridiculous bow tie."

"It wasn't ridiculous. It had tiny seahorses on it. Very dignified."

She remembered now—the silk bow tie with its whimsical pattern, how it had softened his serious demeanor, how she'd adjusted it for him just before they left the room, her fingers lingering at his collar.

Emma smiled, the real memory displacing the manufactured one. "Thank you," she said simply.

He didn't pretend to misunderstand. Since her escape from Alex's control, Marcus had become adept at helping her separate truth from fiction, never dismissing her confusion, always ready to provide the authentic history she sometimes still struggled to grasp.

"Come on," he said, tugging her gently toward the door. "I'll make that spicy crab pasta while you help our budding marine biologist with her specimen preservation."

Inside, the cottage glowed with warm light. Lily had spread newspapers across the kitchen table and arranged her cleaning tools with scientific precision—soft brushes, a magnifying glass, and small containers of solution that Marcus had mixed for her delicate finds. Her expression of intense concentration mirrored Emma's own when examining samples—brows slightly furrowed, lips pressed together, eyes narrowed in focus.

"Did you know," Lily announced without looking up as they entered, "that sand dollars have five sets of pores arranged like flower petals? That's how they breathe."

"Is that so?" Emma settled beside her daughter, inhaling the comforting scents of their temporary home—driftwood burning in the small fireplace, the lemon oil Marcus used on the pine furniture, the lingering aroma of sea air that permeated everything.

As Marcus moved around the kitchen gathering ingredients, the familiar sounds of his cooking formed a soothing backdrop—the soft thud of the cutting board, the rhythmic chopping of herbs, the hiss of garlic hitting hot oil. Emma guided Lily through the careful cleaning process, their heads bent together over the fragile treasure.

"Gentle strokes, that's it. You don't want to damage the pattern."

"Did you know sand dollars are actually sea urchins?" Lily asked, not looking up from her work. "They're related to starfish too."

"I did know that. They belong to the class Echinoidea. Their mouths are in the center of their underside."

Lily nodded solemnly. "Dad showed me in his book." She paused, then added in a smaller voice, "Did I know that before? When I was with Uncle Alex?"

The question hung in the air like glass, beautiful but dangerous if shattered. Emma's heart contracted painfully. These moments still came occasionally—Lily trying to sort through what had been real during her time under Alex's influence. Dr. Patel had advised them to answer honestly but briefly, without dwelling on the trauma.

"I don't think so, sweetheart. Uncle Alex didn't teach you much about marine biology."

Lily absorbed this with a thoughtful nod, her small fingers still working the soft brush over the sand dollar's surface. "I like knowing things for real." She returned to her work, seemingly satisfied with the answer.

Over her daughter's bent head, Emma met Marcus's gaze across the room. Something passed between them—not just understanding but a deeper bond forged in shared suffering and recovery. Marcus gave her a small smile, then returned to the pasta sauce, adding white wine that sizzled dramatically.

"Can I smell it?" Lily asked, setting down her brush and slipping from her chair. She padded across to Marcus, who lifted her up to peer into the pot.

"Careful of the steam," he warned, one strong arm secure around her waist. "What do you think it needs?"

Lily's face screwed up in concentration as she sniffed. "More pepper," she declared with authority.

"More pepper it is," Marcus agreed solemnly, reaching for the grinder. "The chef has spoken."

Emma watched them, this tableau of father and daughter illuminated by the soft kitchen light. There had been so many moments like
this stolen from them—ordinary, precious interactions that should
have filled Lily's early years. Yet here they were, creating new ones,
reclaiming what Alex had tried to destroy.

After dinner, with Lily tucked into bed surrounded by her books
on ocean creatures, Emma and Marcus stood together at the cottage's
large windows. Night had fully claimed the sky, revealing a scatter of
stars that seemed to mirror the distant lights of fishing boats on the
horizon.

"I finished reading the final deposition today," Emma said, breaking
their comfortable silence. "From Alex's research assistant."

Marcus's body tensed beside her, almost imperceptibly. He didn't
respond immediately, his thumb tracing slow circles against her
shoulder. "And?" he finally asked.

"She confirmed what we suspected. Alex had been developing the
memory compounds for years before he targeted me. There were others—experiments that failed. People who suffered psychotic breaks or
complete memory loss." Emma swallowed hard. "She said he became
fixated on me after seeing my documentary series. Called me 'the
perfect subject.'"

The words felt bitter on her tongue, the thought of being reduced
to a laboratory specimen making her skin crawl even now. The deposition had been clinical, detached—pages of testimony describing
how Alexander Sterling had meticulously planned her abduction, calculated dosages, maintained detailed records of her responses to the
compounds.

"Emma—" Marcus began, his voice tight with concern. "No, it's
okay. I needed to know." She turned to face him, tracing the outline

of his face in the dim light. "What I still don't understand is why. Why go to such lengths?"

Marcus sighed, his forehead creasing. "My brother always needed to control things. Even as kids, he couldn't stand when situations evolved naturally. He'd manipulate games, relationships, anything to create the outcome he'd decided was correct."

"But to drug me for years, to erase my memories and replace them with false ones, to steal our child—" Emma shook her head. "It goes beyond control."

The cruelty of it still staggered her—how meticulously Alex had constructed her prison, a cage made not of bars but of altered perceptions. She had lived five years believing she was married to him, that they had conceived Lily together, that Marcus was a dangerous obsessive who threatened their family. The level of calculation required chilled her to the core.

"The prosecution psychiatrist called it 'malignant possession,'" Marcus said quietly. "He didn't just want to control you. He wanted to own you completely—your past, present, future. Your very identity."

Emma shivered despite the warmth of the room. "What would have happened if I hadn't started to remember? If I hadn't found those letters?"

Marcus's expression darkened, shadows gathering in the hollows of his face. "Let's not think about that." He gently tucked a strand of hair behind her ear, his fingers lingering against her cheek. "You did remember. You found your way back. That's what matters."

Emma nodded, though the thought of those lost years still ached like a phantom limb. The horror of it sometimes threatened to overwhelm her, especially in quiet moments when her guard was down.

"I'm going for a walk," she decided suddenly. "Just to the lighthouse and back."

Concern flickered across Marcus's face. "It's getting late. The path is dark."

"I'll take the big flashlight," Emma insisted, already reaching for her jacket. "I just need some air. To clear my head."

After a moment's hesitation, Marcus nodded. "Want company?"

"Not this time." She pressed a quick kiss to his lips, feeling him respond with gentle pressure. "I won't be long. Just need to sort some thoughts."

Outside, the night air carried the tang of salt and approaching rain. Emma switched on the powerful beam of the flashlight, illuminating the worn path that wound from their cottage to the lighthouse. The beacon swept overhead in its eternal rhythm, creating moving shadows that danced across the rocky ground.

The path narrowed as it climbed, forcing Emma to watch her footing. Loose stones shifted beneath her shoes, and the wind grew stronger as she ascended, whipping her hair across her face. Yet the physical exertion felt good—a simple challenge with a clear solution, unlike the tangled mess of her recovered memories.

When she reached the base of the lighthouse, Emma paused, tilting her head back to observe the massive structure against the night sky. During her captivity with Alex, this lighthouse had appeared in her dreams—a symbol her subconscious had used to guide her toward truth.

She circled to the ocean-facing side, where a small bench had been installed for visitors. Settling onto the weathered wood, Emma switched off her flashlight. Darkness enveloped her, broken only by the steady sweep of the light above and the distant glimmer of stars.

The sound of waves crashing against the rocks below filled the night, a constant rhythm that matched her breathing. Slowly, Emma allowed the memories to surface—not Alex's carefully constructed falsehoods, but the painful truth she had been reclaiming piece by piece.

She remembered now how it had started: meeting Marcus first, falling in love with his quiet intensity and brilliant mind; encountering Alex later at a medical conference where she was speaking about ocean conservation; the way his interest had seemed professional at first, then increasingly personal despite her gentle rejections.

The harassment that followed—calls, unexpected appearances, gifts she returned. Then the joy of discovering she was pregnant with Marcus's child, followed by the escalating threats from Alex. The restraining order that had driven him temporarily away.

And finally, the night that had changed everything. Marcus away on a research vessel in the North Atlantic. Emma, eight months pregnant, waking to find Alex in her bedroom with a syringe. The violation of that moment—the chemical stealing her consciousness, her will, her very self—remained the most horrifying memory of all.

Emma pressed her hands against the rough wood of the bench, anchoring herself in the present. That was over now. Alex was locked away in a psychiatric facility for the criminally insane, his medical license revoked, his research discredited. He would never touch her again, never manipulate her mind or threaten her family.

Yet still, on nights like this, Emma wondered about those lost years. What experiences had been stolen from her forever? Lily's first steps, first words, first day of school—all consumed by Alex's obsession, replaced with manufactured moments featuring himself in the role meant for Marcus.

The sound of footsteps on the path drew her from these dark thoughts. Emma tensed momentarily, her hand reaching for the flashlight, before a familiar voice called out.

"Emma? Are you up there?"

Marcus's tall figure appeared at the edge of the lighthouse clearing, his own flashlight beam bobbing as he approached.

"I thought you were staying at the cottage," she said as he drew closer.

"I was. Then Lily woke up and insisted we both come find you." He gestured behind him, where Lily stood in her jacket thrown over pajamas, her own small flashlight clutched tightly.

"She had a dream," Marcus explained. "Said we needed to be together at the lighthouse."

Lily approached, her expression solemn in the dim light. "I dreamed about the bad doctor," she said simply. "But then the lighthouse made him go away."

Emma opened her arms, and Lily climbed onto her lap, a warm weight against her chest. "The lighthouse is our protector, isn't it?" Emma murmured into her daughter's hair.

"That's what you always said," Lily confirmed. "Even when we were with Uncle Alex, you used to tell me bedtime stories about the magic lighthouse that would guide lost sailors home."

Emma's breath caught. Another piece of the puzzle clicked into place—how she had managed to preserve some truth even within Alex's carefully controlled environment, passing hidden messages to her daughter through stories he would have dismissed as childish fantasy.

"Your mom is very clever," Marcus said, settling beside them on the bench. "She always finds a way to shine light into dark places."

Together, the three of them sat watching the lighthouse beam circle endlessly overhead. The wind carried hints of the coming storm—not a threat now, but a cleansing force that would wash the world clean by morning.

The vast darkness of the ocean stretched before them, mysterious and powerful. Yet Emma felt no fear—only a growing certainty that they had weathered the worst storm of all and emerged intact, if changed.

When Lily's eyelids began to droop, Marcus gently lifted her into his arms. The child nestled against his chest, her breathing deepening into sleep. Emma rose, brushing sand from her jeans, and slipped her hand into Marcus's free one.

"Ready to go home?" he whispered.

Emma looked up at him, at the lines of worry and love etched into his face by all they had endured. In the sweep of the lighthouse beam, his eyes caught the light, reflecting back at her with an intensity that made her heart quicken.

"Yes," she said softly. "I'm ready."

www.ingramcontent.com/pod-product-compliance
Lightning Source LLC
Chambersburg PA
CBHW011435240626
47153CB00011B/3007